J FIC White
White, Kiersten.
Wretched waterpark

DC - Nov 2023

S0-AEN-366

WRETCHED
WATERPARK

THE SINISTER SUMMER SERIES

WRETCHED WATERPARK

Kiersten White

DELACORTE PRESS

This is a work of fiction. Names, characters, places, and incidents either are the product of the author's imagination or are used fictitiously. Any resemblance to actual persons, living or dead, events, or locales is entirely coincidental.

Text copyright © 2022 by Kiersten Brazier
Jacket art copyright © 2022 by Hannah Peck

All rights reserved. Published in the United States by Delacorte Press, an imprint of Random House Children's Books, a division of Penguin Random House LLC, New York.

Delacorte Press is a registered trademark and the colophon is a trademark of Penguin Random House LLC.

rhcbooks.com

Educators and librarians, for a variety of teaching tools, visit us at RHTeachersLibrarians.com

Library of Congress Cataloging-in-Publication Data
Names: White, Kiersten, author.
Title: Wretched waterpark / Kiersten White.
Description: First edition. | New York : Delacorte Press, [2022] | Series: The sinister summer series | Audience: Ages 8–12. | Summary: Twins Theo and Alexander and their sister Wil are abruptly dropped off at their Aunt Saffronia's house, where they learn they must complete a series of tasks in order to see their parents again—and their first assignment is at a waterpark.
Identifiers: LCCN 2021012608 (print) | LCCN 2021012609 (ebook) | ISBN 978-0-593-37904-2 (hardcover) | ISBN 978-0-593-37906-6 (ebook) | ISBN 978-0-593-57258-0 (int'l edition)
Subjects: CYAC: Brothers and sisters—Fiction. | Twins—Fiction. | Amusement parks—Fiction. | Missing persons—Fiction. | Mystery and detective stories. | LCGFT: Novels. | Detective and mystery fiction.
Classification: LCC PZ7.W583764 Wr 2022 (print) | LCC PZ7.W583764 (ebook) | DDC [Fic]—dc23

The text of this book is set in 12.75-point Adobe Jenson Pro.
Interior design by Jen Valero

Printed in the United States of America
10 9 8 7 6 5 4 3 2 1
First Edition

Random House Children's Books supports the First Amendment and celebrates the right to read.

Penguin Random House LLC supports copyright. Copyright fuels creativity, encourages diverse voices, promotes free speech, and creates a vibrant culture. Thank you for buying an authorized edition of this book and for complying with copyright laws by not reproducing, scanning, or distributing any part in any form without permission. You are supporting writers and allowing Penguin Random House to publish books for every reader.

To all the kids afraid of the deep end:
Same.

WRETCHED
WATERPARK

og drifted around their feet, clinging greedily, like it wanted to pull them into a watery grave.

And maybe, this being the worst summer ever, it would actually end that way.

"To save Wil," Theo whispered.

"To save our friends," Alexander whispered.

"To save—well, let's just do those two first and worry about the rest if we survive." Theo was always practical that way. Her brother nodded. They clutched each other's hands and took a deep breath. Then they jumped into the pool, glowing green and hungry beneath them. Their dark hair floated behind them as they sank, slowly, to the bottom, took a few steps . . .

And then disappeared.

CHAPTER
ONE

Their aunt was decidedly Sinister.

But only because she was from their mother's side of the family. If she had been from their father's side of the family, she would have been decidedly Winterbottom. It had been a great trial for each of the Sinister-Winterbottom children to learn how to write their own names, something their usually thoughtful parents had neglected to think through.

Another thing their parents had neglected to think through was the wisdom of dropping off sixteen-year-old Wilhelmina Sinister-Winterbottom (who had actually learned how to write her own name as a toddler), twelve-year-old Theodora Sinister-Winterbottom (who had never to this day written out her whole name, preferring Theo), and *also* twelve-year-old Alexander Sinister-Winterbottom (who had always insisted on each and every letter of his entire name and would not answer to Alex even if he were hanging off the side of a cliff and a search party was frantically shouting it) to spend the summer with their aunt Saffronia Sinister, whom the children had never met, and who, by all appearances, had never encountered an actual human child before.

Wil had been adopted as a baby. Theo and Alexander had joined the family four years later, born hand in hand. Sometimes, still, when they weren't paying attention or they were nervous or scared, they reached for each other's hands.

They weren't reaching for each other's hands now, though, because they weren't nervous or scared. Just confused. Their noses—with matching freckles dotted across quick-to-sunburn white skin—wrinkled in unison.

"Do you remember getting here?" Alexander whispered.

"What?" Theo answered, shifting closer to him. Her short, spiky brown hair was pushed back from her forehead with a headband. Alexander's was neatly combed and gelled into place.

"How did we get here?"

"The kitchen?"

"No, this house, in— Where are we? What town is this, Aunt Saffronia?"

But Aunt Saffronia spoke as though she didn't hear Alexander's question. "I wonder about your parents' judgment, summoning *me*. I am not well suited to—" Aunt Saffronia gestured vaguely in their direction. "And I wonder if you will be suited to the grave tasks ahead. Still. They had no other options."

"So you're taking care of us. The whole summer." Theo scowled.

Aunt Saffronia merely nodded. "How often would you say you need to eat? If I set out some food in the morning, will that be enough?"

"Depends on how much food you set out," Wil answered, not bothering to look up from where she tapped furiously on the screen of her phone. Her fingers moved so fast, sometimes they blurred. Her phone's name was Rodrigo, and it was her third-favorite member of the family. She always refused to say who were in first and second place, though, leaving Alexander vaguely worried that he came in after the phone. Theo was confident she was first and would not have believed it if anyone had told her otherwise.

"It also depends on what kind of food you set out," added Alexander, who was very particular about food-safety protocols. Images of sweating cartons of milk going sour made him feel as though he were breaking out in a cold sweat along with the milk.

"Definitely not enough," said Theo. "We need to eat at least as often as you do."

Aunt Saffronia pursed her colorless lips. This statement seemed to puzzle her even more than trying to calculate how to feed three children. "Yes. As often as I . . . eat."

Theo stomped past her and opened the fridge. It was empty. Apparently the food in question was theoretical. And theoretical food was Theo's least favorite type. She even preferred beets over theoretical food, and all beets tasted like dirt.

Alexander was distracted from the theoretical food by the non-theoretical kitchen. It looked like it had been transported directly from an old TV show. The floor was black-and-white tile, the walls a warm marigold color, the cabinets and counters white like the old-fashioned fridge. Had he not still been vaguely queasy just thinking about spoiled milk, he would have appreciated how well the kitchen matched his aunt.

Aunt Saffronia looked a bit like she had been transported from another era as well. Her dress trailed on the floor, hiding her feet. Her hair was long and straight, nearly black, and her skin was so pale it blended in with the stark white cabinets. Her large eyes, which Alexander was fairly certain had not blinked once during this conversation, remained fixed on a point somewhere behind them.

"I could . . . buy some food?" she suggested. Alexander did not understand why it was a question and not a statement.

"Or you could order it," Wil said, scowling at Rodrigo. If Aunt Saffronia never blinked, Wil never looked up from the shiny screen.

"How?"

"On your phone."

Aunt Saffronia looked at an odd sculpture affixed to one wall. She picked up part of the sculpture and held it gingerly to her ear. It was, puzzlingly, a phone. Why was it on the wall? Why did it have that curly cord, like a leash keeping it in one place? Was it going to run away if it were set loose?

"Hello?" Aunt Saffronia whispered. "Is anyone there? Do you have food?"

Wil finally looked up. "I mean on your cell phone? Using the internet?" She shook Rodrigo meaningfully. Her fingernails were bright blue, her skin was dark brown, and her face held an expression Theo and Alexander both knew meant she was about to lose it. Their parents would have gently redirected her to the piano to slam out her anger on the keys, but their parents weren't here, and neither was their piano, and neither was anything from home, because their parents had decided to ruin the entire summer.

Why? The kids had been roused from their beds in the middle of the night with urgency. Urgency and candles. A *lot* of candles. Why had their parents been lighting so many candles? Then—they were here. Alexander couldn't quite fill in the blanks. Had they taken a car? An airplane? A train? Why couldn't he remember?

But he remembered the worry behind his parents' eyes as they tried to smile and promise the summer would be great. He couldn't shake that same worry, like it had jumped from them to him, like it was connected to him with the same tangled, curling leash that kept the phone on the wall.

He didn't think this summer would be great.

In the absence of a piano, Theo stepped in. She wasn't worried. She was annoyed. She'd had big plans for this summer, and now they were all on hold. "Do you have a cell phone?" she asked, wanting to study the antique phone she had thought was merely decorative. The whole thing was absurd but kind of funny, and she wondered how it worked. "Or a computer?"

"What's the Wi-Fi password? I can't find a signal." Wil's fingers tightened around Rodrigo.

"Water park!" Aunt Saffronia said, a smile like a skull's grimace on her face. "I'm taking you children to the water park. It's the first task to be accomplished."

"We have to accomplish a water park?" Alexander asked.

"What does 'task' even mean? Isn't that like an assignment?" Theo chimed in. "Do you mean 'activity'?"

"And besides," Aunt Saffronia said, ignoring their questions once again, "children like water. And parks."

"Does the water park have Wi-Fi?" Wil asked through gritted teeth.

"Does the water park have food?" Theo asked.

"Does the water park have strict food-safety protocols and an A rating from the local health department?" Alexander asked.

None of them asked if the water park was plagued with a series of mysterious disappearances, which would soon be much more important to them than Wi-Fi or lunch, but, in Alexander's case, would still rank slightly below food-safety protocols.

CHAPTER
TWO

"Here we are!" Aunt Saffronia sounded as relieved as the three Sinister-Winterbottoms felt as they tumbled out of her ancient metal beast of a car. She drifted along the roads in the same way she drifted through her house—distracted, never quite focused, and with an air of confused distance. None of which were ideal qualities in a driver.

Aunt Saffronia rolled down her window. Though the day was windy, her hair did not move. "Get the week pass. A week should be enough time."

"Enough time for what?" Theo asked.

"Yes, exactly. We need time. We don't have it yet, but we must get it. Do you understand?"

"Really, really no," Alexander said. Wil wasn't even listening, but Theo looked as confused as Alexander felt.

"*Find what was lost,*" Aunt Saffronia said, and there was something strange about her voice—it went from sounding sort of like an echo, to sounding like a rumble of thunder. Theo and Alexander *felt* it. They both nodded without quite knowing why.

"Very good. I'll pick you up when it gets dark," Aunt Saffronia said, her eyes fixed on a point far above their heads. "Outside, I mean. It might get dark in many ways far before then, but you are good, brave children." She drove away without another word.

"Fantastic," Wil said, not looking up from Rodrigo. "A week at a water park. If our aunt wasn't going to bother watching us, why didn't Mom and Dad just let me be in charge?"

"I'm gonna walk into traffic now," Theo said, testing her.

"Hey, Theo," Alexander said. "Do you think this knife is sharp enough? Here, hold out your hand."

Wil had not heard a word, thus proving why, exactly, their parents did not leave her in charge. Perhaps if Theo and Alexander had *texted* Wil that they were going to get matching tattoos or were ingesting poisons in small doses to increase their tolerance, she might have responded.

But probably not.

"Why do you think they left us with Aunt Saffronia?" Alexander asked. "And do any of you remember her ever being mentioned? Wil, have you met her before?"

Wil just grunted noncommittally. "I'm busy," she said, fingers tapping.

"I don't really listen when Dad talks about his family, and Mom never talks about hers." Theo shrugged.

"Doesn't that seem weird? That Mom never, ever talks about her family, but suddenly we're with a Sinister aunt? Is she Mom's sister? Married to one of Mom's brothers or sisters? Does Mom even have any brothers or sisters? And doesn't Aunt Saffronia seem . . . ?"

"Too old?" Theo suggested.

But that wasn't it. She didn't look old, like as in wrinkly and decrepit. She looked old like a photograph you find in a box, youth captured but frozen and faded, long gone even though it's right in front of you. Alexander opened his mouth to share that thought, but Theo had already moved on. She liked movement and hated standing still.

"So, the water park," Theo said, hands on her hips as she slowly turned in a circle. "Where exactly is it?"

Aunt Saffronia had dropped them on the side of the road. The trees were old, green and gray, heavy with trailing Spanish moss. A few steps into their shade lowered the temperature by several degrees. The only thing they could see was a gravel road leading into the forest.

Alexander rubbed his arms against the sudden chill. "Maybe along this road?"

Theo went confidently in that direction, followed by Alexander and less quickly by Wil, who navigated much like a bat with echolocation, only without the echolocation. She stumbled on the occasional root and walked directly into at least one tree, neither action peeling her eyes away from her phone.

Theo ran her hand through her hair, making it stick up wildly. She had been trying for low-maintenance, and ended up looking a bit like a young, brunette Albert Einstein. "It's a sign," she said.

Alexander thought she was being metaphorical, referring to their being lost in the woods as a sign that their entire summer was doomed, until he followed her gaze upward to an *actual* sign.

In rusting wrought-iron, curling and twisting more

elaborately than the ivy trailing from it, a gate stood. Along the top in imposingly sharp letters was written:

FATHOMS OF FUN WATERPARK

Wil's eyes flicked up and then back down. "It has five stars on . . . Gulp. Not Yelp. Gulp. I've never heard of Gulp." Unconcerned, she continued walking forward, missing the edge of the gate by a hair.

Alexander hiked his backpack up, tightening the straps. He didn't like water parks, or parks in general, though he was fond of water. Still, the sign felt more ominous than exciting. And decidedly un-water-parkish.

Theo loved water parks, and parks in general, and she was also very fond of water. "Race you," Theo said.

"Race yourself," Alexander answered.

Theo obliged, as she always did. She took off sprinting along the gravel road, pumping her legs and arms in perfect unison. She was very good at running, and climbing, and swimming. She was rather bad at sitting still, waiting, and spelling. Unlike Wil and Alexander, she was excited by the prospect of a week at a water park. With a full week, she could do all sorts of things. Time herself going down slides and aim for new personal records, adjusting for friction, body positioning, even the time of day. Make a course out of the slides and race Alexander to see who could get through fastest. And have a churro-eating contest. Last summer she'd been introduced to those delightful lengths of fried-dough-cinnamon-sugar goodness, and they tasted like *happiness*, like what summer vacation felt like. She was confident she would win any churro-eating contests. And it could impact her slide times in interesting ways!

All her thoughts of churro consumption came to a screeching halt as her sneakers slid on the gravel and she stopped just short of the entrance gates.

Wil and Alexander caught up. Wil kept walking. Alexander stopped next to his twin and stared.

Water parks are this:

The scents of chlorine, sunscreen, and water drying on pavement.

Sun-drenched bright colors—yellow and blue mostly, some red. Palm trees, real or fake. Rainbow-colored shade umbrellas. Aqua slides like twisty straws for giants.

Children running and laughing and screaming and crying, parents likely doing the same minus the laughing, everyone in tropical-print suits, board shorts, bikinis, wraps.

Somehow, Fathoms of Fun had entirely missed the meeting where water parks were explained. Theo and Alexander would have been sure it wasn't a water park at all, except for the sign—carved in the base of a giant angel statue, the wings thrown forward to hide the angel's face—listing prices for entrance, including suit and towel rentals. The prices were all listed in roman numerals.

"Whoa," Theo said. "Do we have XVII dollars?"

"Yes," Alexander said. "But do we want to have it, if it means we're going inside *there*?"

Beyond the massive ivy-choked stone wall, beyond the wrought-iron gate slowly swinging open as if beckoning them in, was a tower. The tower loomed above the overhanging green trees, scraping against the sky itself. Rather than wood scaffolding, or even metal or plastic, the tower was made of the same heavy, weather-pocked gray stone of the wall. At various points along the tower, huge gargoyle heads leered, and between their jaws, gray slides extended like lolling tongues, twisting and looping away. At the very top of the tower, where one half expected either a lighthouse light or a cannon, there was a window. Theo frowned, thinking she saw a flash of white there, a hand pressed against the glass. But it was too far away to be sure.

"Come on," Wil said, annoyed. She stood in front of the ticket window. Unlike most ticket windows, it was actually a window with a stained-glass scene of a stormy sea and a woman in white staring out at the waves. Alexander could almost smell the tang of salt in the air, could almost feel the charge before lightning.

Theo could almost taste churros, could almost feel the thrill of free-falling down a slide. As weird as that tower was, it was *tall*. She was ready.

A woman passed them, walking away from the park, bag slung over her shoulder, child's hand firmly grasped in her own. "We'll find something else to do today," she said to her son, who didn't seem sad to be walking away from a water park rather than into it. "*Anything* else."

The ticket window swung open. "Can I help you?"

In place of a lanky teenager wearing a park-branded tank top, there was a woman in a long-sleeved dress with a lace collar so high it came up around her chin, making it look as though her head was being served on a platter. She had a face like a sheet of plastic wrap over a bowl of mashed potatoes. Her eyebrows were drawn on in harsh black, one of which seemed to meander a little too far down the side of her face, as though it had forgotten what it set off to do. Even though the day was cloudy and the ticket booth was shaded, she wore large, dark glasses. They had reflective green lenses that made her eyes impossible to see.

"One adult and two child week passes, please," Wil said, sliding the credit card their parents got for her forward while tapping furiously on Rodrigo.

The woman frowned. "Are you certain this is what you want?"

"Yes," Wil said.

The woman's head swiveled, and she fixed her unnervingly eyeless gaze on Theo and Alexander. "Think of the children. Think of their happiness. Their safety. Are you *certain* this is what you want?"

"Yeah, yeah, I got them. I'm old enough to supervise, thanks."

Theo and Alexander realized they were grasping hands. Something about those odd lenses made what the woman was saying sound less like a caution and more like a threat.

"We can both swim," Alexander chirped, his voice coming out higher and more worried than he had intended. Adults usually liked him, and he liked being liked.

"Competitively," Theo said, her jaw clenched and her eyes narrowed. She never noticed whether or not adults liked her, but she hated being treated like a child.

"Very well. Please sign this last will and testament."

Finally, Wil looked up. "What?"

"Waiver," the woman corrected. "Liability waiver. It means you cannot sue us should you be injured either physically or emotionally during your time here."

"Emotionally injured?" Theo asked.

"And if you were to perish, you could not sue us in either this life or the next."

Wil held out her hand for a pen. "Sure. Fine. Do you have Wi-Fi?"

"Yes."

"Can I get the password?"

"One," the woman said.

Wil typed it in and waited.

"Two."

Wil typed it in and waited.

"Three."

Wil typed it in and waited.

"Four."

Wil typed it in and waited.

"Five."

Wil typed it in and waited.

"Six."

Wil typed it in and waited.

"Seven."

Wil typed it in and said, "Eight?"

"Oh, blast," the woman said, scowling. "Now I've lost my place because you interrupted me. Sign the waiver while I find where they've written the password."

In place of a ballpoint pen attached to a chain, the woman pulled out a quill and dipped it into a jar of black ink.

"Groovy aesthetic you have going on here." Wil took the quill, signed her name, and passed it to Theo. Theo signed, then passed it to Alexander. Alexander looked down at the paper—more like parchment—which was filled with what appeared to be handwritten warnings. He caught a few words, including *terror, long-lost relatives, drowning accidental or otherwise,* and *not responsible for lost items or souls.* But Theo and Wil had already signed.

"They have to do these," Theo said, unworried but noticing that Alexander was un-unworried. He was always worrying about things she really didn't think he should be. "I've signed hundreds of them for track and swim meets. It doesn't mean anything, just that lawyers make them do it. They couldn't have a water park that wasn't safe. It would get shut down."

"It would, wouldn't it?" The woman had reappeared, and her smile was as sharp as a shark's.

Alexander swallowed against the lump in his throat. He wanted to take his time and read every line of the waiver, but Theo nudged him and he signed his name.

"Here's the Wi-Fi password," the woman announced, sliding forward a worn sheet on which was written 1 2 3 4 5 6 7 8. Then she took the waiver and pulled it into the darkness of the booth.

"Riiiiiight. So do we need wristbands or what?" Wil asked. She was already angled toward the entrance, phone leading the way.

The woman held out three heavy brass lockets. "Please wear these at all times. Do not remove them. We cannot be held responsible if you remove it and are lost. I mean if you remove it and are lost. I mean—" She frowned. "Just don't remove it."

"Old-school," Wil muttered, fastening hers around her neck. "And it doesn't go with my suit."

Alexander put his on, the metal cold and heavy around his neck. Theo couldn't get hers to clasp, but she didn't want to waste time, so she ended up tying it on when no one was looking. She'd fix it later.

It wasn't that Theo wasn't also worried about why her parents had woken them in the middle of the night and then just . . . disappeared, but she could never figure out how to *feel* things like that. When things felt too big, her insides got all scattered and buzzing, like she was full of bees. She hated it, so she channeled big feelings into movement and action. And since she couldn't force her parents to come back, that movement and action would have to be used going down some amazing waterslides.

The woman pointed at the park. "Your pass comes with a mausoleum, where you can leave your belongings and retreat into the shadows."

"Sorry, did you say mausoleum?" Alexander asked. He knew that word. A mausoleum was a fancy miniature building where people kept coffins. And coffins were where people kept *dead bodies*.

"No," the woman answered. "Cabana. I said 'cabana.' 'Cabana' and 'mausoleum' sound very similar."

Theo raised her eyebrows. "Yeah, I get those two confused all the time."

The woman's smile didn't move as she reached out

one clawlike hand and slowly drew the window shut once more. "Cabana number thirteen," she said. "Good luck."

"That's weird, right?" Alexander asked as they turned to follow Wil into the park.

"Which part?" Theo asked, bouncing on the balls of her feet. They had been standing still for way too long and the bees in her chest were *buzzing*.

"The part where all of it?"

"Yup. Super weird. Race you to the cabana!"

For once, Alexander was game, if only to make certain he wasn't left by himself. They took off running, darting around the stone wall edge.

Two hands, clad in black gloves, shot out of the shadows and grabbed the twins.

CHAPTER THREE

As usual, when something unexpected happened, Theo was the first to respond. And she responded with her feet, kicking out hard at the shins that belonged to the legs that belonged to the torso that belonged to the arms that belonged to the hands that belonged to the person who had grabbed them, dragging them into the shadows of an ivy-covered alcove.

"Leggo!" Theo shouted.

"Please?" Alexander added, because it felt like he should counteract Theo's kicking and demanding. Best to cover all their bases.

The black-clad hands released them, and they

stared up and up and up into the face of the tallest person they had ever seen. He was gaunt and pale, neck bent like a turkey—or perhaps a vulture, with beady, deep-set eyes to match. "Turkey vulture," Alexander whispered, remembering the summer a whole wake of turkey vultures had descended on their neighborhood. He had been scared at first, until his mother encouraged him to research them. It turned out they were actually pretty cool, if still a bit unsettling to look at.

Perhaps this man would prove to be the same, but Alexander didn't have high hopes. The turkey-vulture man pulled his hands back into his sleeves and seemed to shrink into his high, starched collar. "You should never run," he said, his voice a scratchy whisper, like the sound of rat claws running over wooden floorboards beneath your bed in the middle of the night. "That's how people disappear."

Alexander frowned. They were in trouble, and he hated being in trouble, but he wasn't certain this man was a lifeguard. Or that the man understood what, exactly, the danger of running on wet surfaces was. "Don't you mean we shouldn't run because that's how people fall and get hurt?"

The man shook his head, his neck skin wobbling

with the movement. "No, that's how people disappear. They are always running first. And then they are gone. So please, children. Please. Walk. And be ever so careful that you, too, do not vanish." He took a step back and was swallowed by the ivy.

Theo and Alexander looked at each other, eyebrows raised. Their eyebrows were getting a very good workout today.

"Maybe we should leave," Alexander said. "Or at least call Mom and Dad and tell them where we are."

Theo scowled. "If they wanted to know where we were, they shouldn't have ditched us."

"Come on," Wil said, drifting past them. They scrambled to catch up—careful not to run this time, in case the turkey-vulture man was still watching them. "Look for a store," Wil said, contradicting herself by not looking for anything other than her phone screen. "We don't have any sunscreen."

It was hard to tell what was a store and what wasn't. The buildings were gray stone, looming overhead as though bullying the children, with elaborate scrolling stonework and leering gargoyles that watched them as they walked by.

All the heavy wooden doors were closed. Many

looked as if they couldn't even open, covered in the same ivy that had swallowed the vulture man. "There!" Theo said, pointing. One of the buildings had a door that was open and a hand-painted sign hanging above it that said "Items and Sundries."

"Do you think sundries is a pun? Like, things to use when you're in the sun?" Alexander asked. He loved wordplay.

Theo frowned. "Doesn't really seem like a punny location, does it?"

To cheer himself up, Alexander vowed to view it as a pun, regardless, and stepped into the building while Theo shouted to get Wil's attention before she wandered away. Inside the store, the walls were paneled in rich, dark wood. The space above the paneling was the same stone as all the building exteriors but painted white. There were several couches—though Alexander felt certain they had a fancier name than *couch*, since they didn't resemble anything he had ever sat on before. Or, frankly, would ever feel comfortable sitting on. He suspected that the moment he put his bottom on that material, the ticket-booth woman would appear to glare at him in disapproval.

Theo, on the other hand, immediately plopped onto

the deep red velvet of the nearest couch. If there were things for sale in here, she couldn't see them. There was a large fireplace with a roaring fire in one corner, a closed door, and several large, freestanding cupboards. Theo was pretty sure they were called armoires, a word she much preferred. It just sounded tougher than cupboards. Like, sure, armoires will hold your things, but they'll *also* stand at your side in battle. The armoires stood at attention imposingly along the walls. A table in the center of the room was lined with glass domes, under which were various displays.

Alexander leaned close to see pinned butterflies, metallic beetles, and . . . goggles. Not the usual plastic neon swimming goggles. These were green-tinted glass, with heavy leather and rubber straps.

"You need help," a voice intoned, startling Alexander and Theo but not startling Wil, because in order to be startled, she would have had to notice that the room had previously been empty, which, eyes glued to Rodrigo, she had not.

Wil didn't look up, her back turned to them. "We need towels, and they need sunscreen." Aunt Saffronia had seemed as puzzled by their request for towels as she had by their requirements for daily meals. At least they had all found their swimsuits in their suitcases, which none of them remembered packing. Their parents must have done that for them.

"Right. Yes. Let me see what we have." The young man, who looked to be around Wil's age, peered at them through his round glasses. He was wearing a charcoal-gray suit with a vest, jacket, and something not quite like a tie but more like a very fancy scarf pinned under his collar.

There was a British show their mother liked called *Harfordshropshireton Manor* where everyone was fancy all the time, including the servants. The shop employee looked like he had wandered out of that show, rather than a more appropriately themed show Wil often watched, the title of which Alexander could never remember but which Theo referred to as *Sunshine Beach People Kiss Each Other and Sometimes Have to Punch People*.

"Do you have towel color preferences?" the fancy young man asked. "We have black, nearly black, and extremely black."

Wil waved dismissively. "Whatever is fine."

The young man pulled out a heavy brass key ring and unlocked one of the looming armoires.

"Do you think that one leads to Narnia?" Theo whispered.

"I think it leads to Hades," Alexander answered.

"Or Castle Dracula."

"Or Frankenstein's laboratory."

"Ah, yes," the young man said, smiling. He had a pleasant smile, brown skin complemented by his purple scarf-tie thing, and straight black hair. "I thought we had some in here, just the right size." He pulled out two long sticks wrapped in black lace.

"What . . . are those?" Theo asked.

"Sun protection." He waited as though it was obvious what the sticks were for, but when Theo and Alexander continued to look confused, he shrugged. "Bad luck, but we certainly can't have any more here than we already do." He untied a ribbon, and with a flick of his wrist, an umbrella revealed itself. A black lace umbrella.

"A parasol?" Alexander asked, aghast.

"A pair of something, all right," Theo said.

"Yes! Best sun protection." The clerk modeled it, holding the cane against his shoulder so the lace loomed over him like an elegant storm cloud.

"But . . . we're going to be swimming." Theo gestured behind herself toward the water park. At this point, she

31

had yet to see any actual water, though. So maybe they wouldn't be swimming. She was trying not to feel annoyed, but the longer she went without flinging herself down a waterslide, the harder it was. The bees were nearing a swarm.

"Well, of course you wouldn't take it in the river or down a slide. There are parasol stands at the entrances to every attraction. Now, towels." He clapped his hands together, peering over his glasses at the selection of armoires before hurrying over to one and unlocking it with a different large brass key. His key ring was filled with them. It had to weigh several pounds, at least.

"Here we are." He pulled out three folded bundles. They were all black, and looked like the same stiff velvet material as the couches. The material had delicate patterns. "Oh, no. Not this one. This one was . . ." He trailed off, looking at one of the towels mournfully, then folded it and placed it on the table apart from the others. He grabbed one that apparently didn't trigger an emotional crisis, added it to the first two, and placed the parasols on top of them.

"That will be, uh . . ." He frowned down at the items, scratching his head. "Well, honestly, I'm not sure. This is my first day in the store. I'm usually ferrying at the

River Styx. Why don't we say . . . ?" He looked up and Wil looked up at the same time, and for some reason they both froze as though very, very frightened or very, very shocked.

"Hi," Wil said, slightly breathless. "I'm Wil."

"Edgar. These are free." He grabbed the towels and parasols and shoved them at Alexander and Theo, never taking his eyes off Wil.

Wil's phone chimed, but she didn't look down. Alexander felt a spike of fear. Was there something wrong? Wil never didn't look at her phone.

"Why don't you guys go find cabana thirteen?" she said, leaning against the back of the nearest couch. "I'm going to, uh, browse for a little bit. If that's okay?"

"I guess," Alexander answered, before realizing she wasn't asking if it was okay with them. She was asking if it was okay with Edgar, who was nodding so fast his tie-scarf was in danger of coming unpinned.

"Okay, cool," Theo said. "A man outside offered us candy and asked us to get in his van, if that's fine with you."

"Yeah, whatever," Wil said, waving in their general direction.

"Best babysitter ever," Theo grumbled. She had been hoping Wil would race her down the slides. She didn't

33

have high hopes for Alexander. She turned and marched back outside. Alexander took the supplies and hurried after her.

They followed the cobblestone walkway, the over-hanging trees so thick that the sun barely touched the ground. Maybe they really wouldn't need sunscreen, which was good, because apparently there wasn't any here. And Alexander wasn't sure he was up for how silly he would look carrying a black lace umbrella.

"Do you smell that?" Theo asked.

"Smell what?"

"No chlorine. It smells like . . ."

"The ocean," Alexander finished. They didn't live near the beach, but they had been enough times to know the heavy salt scent of the sea. At last they came around a bend and saw a series of small, open buildings along a rocky entrance to a pool. Instead of bright white and blue, the bottom of the pool was black stone. It looked *cold*. Waves pushed against the edges, foaming and restless. A looming cave swallowed the waves when they retreated, claiming them in darkness, though a hint of lumines-cence glowed through.

"Thirteen," Theo declared, pointing. The cabanas, lined up in a row and entirely empty, didn't look like cabanas. They weren't wood, or tents, or really anything that said "Sunshine!" or "Fun!" or even "Living humans!"

They were, in fact, mausoleums. Or at least designed to look like them. Theo and Alexander's parents had often taken them to a very old family cemetery. There were several mausoleums made to hold multiple caskets. These looked exactly the same, minus the caskets. At least minus the caskets that Alexander and Theo could see.

Ponderous stone pillars guarded the entrance to each mausoleum, with winged angels at the top. The angels were all in different poses. Some pointed at the pool with looks of horror. Others were on their knees, staring upward as though entreating some higher power to intervene. The angels on their own mausoleum stared down, solemn, their fingers pointing back toward the entrance to the park.

Alexander didn't really want to go inside. He was half-certain there would be actual caskets. But Theo didn't hesitate. She marched inside, claimed by the shadows, and Alexander scurried after her.

Inside, stained-glass windows let in pattered light. There were three lounge chairs—upholstered in that same heavy red velvet that didn't seem like a practical choice for wet bodies. But then again, Alexander had never designed a water park, so he didn't know for certain that they weren't practical. Maybe velvet was the best material for water absorption. Judging by the musty, slightly sour smell inside the mausoleum, though, he highly doubted it.

"This is not a cabana," Alexander said.

"More like a mausona," Theo said.

"Or a cabeum," Alexander said.

"Or," they both said together, eyes lighting up, "a cabasoleum!" They nodded, settled on the correct term for cabana 13, then put their bags down.

"Weird," Theo said, frowning at the back of the tiny building. There was something off about it.

"Which part?" Alexander asked, gesturing to everything around them.

Theo shrugged. She didn't know how to explain that the building was . . . wrong. And besides, she needed to move. She peeled off her pants and shirt to the swimsuit she wore beneath them, leaving her outer clothes on the floor. Alexander set down the towels and parasols and did the same, carefully folding his clothing and setting his things in the corner, rather than on one of the suspiciously musty chairs. He was glad he had decided to wear a swim shirt that went all the way to his wrists, since sunscreen wasn't an option. The shirt was fluorescent green—his mother's idea—and the shorts he wore with it featured a wide variety of sharks. Also his mother's idea. He was personally terrified of sharks—they ranked above avalanches and sinkholes but below improperly followed food-safety protocols on his list of things that kept him up at night—but his mother always said, "Sometimes the best way to overcome our fears is to claim what scares us as our own."

He wasn't sure how cartoon hammerhead sharks swimming around his thighs counted as claiming sharks as his own, but looking down at his shorts made him miss his parents with a sharp sting.

"Come on," Theo said, refusing to miss their parents. She didn't want to, so she wasn't going to. "We're wasting the day!"

Alexander hurried out in front of her so he wouldn't be left alone in the mausoleum. She took a step to follow him, then paused. She had the oddest sensation of being watched—from behind. But no one else had been in the mausoleum. She turned slowly, eyes narrowed and fists clenched, but there was only the dim, solid-stone back of the mausoleum. No one was there.

That she could see, anyway.

The eyes they could not see watched as Theo and Alexander spilled out of the mausoleum and into the park.

CHAPTER FOUR

Even brave Theo was unnerved by the yawning black cave of the wave pool, stalactites hanging like teeth waiting to snag them and swallow them whole, waves crashing so hard they receded with foamy violence. No one was in there, either. Sometimes when no one is in a pool, that makes the pool more enticing. In this case, it made Theo feel like maybe there was a reason.

Besides, she wanted speed, not waves. Near the center of the park was a stand—though less a stand and more a minor fortification that could have repelled enemy invasion with only a handful of soldiers. Theo assumed this stand was to give out the tubes for the slides, the pool, and the lazy river.

"Do you have double tubes?" Theo asked, leaning on the counter. She wanted a double so Alexander would have no choice but to join her on the slides. The employee, a woman who looked like a candle that had been left burning too long, shook her head.

Candles reminded Theo of something. She couldn't quite remember what. Her mother used candles sometimes, Christmassy-smelling ones. She always got annoyed when Theo pretended they were birthday candles and blew them out to make a wish. But those weren't the candles Theo was thinking of. The ones she was thinking of hadn't smelled like Christmas. And they had been lit hastily in the middle of the night.

"Do you remember—" she started to ask Alexander, but the woman at the stand spoke, interrupting her.

"No doubles. All fateful journeys must, in the end, be taken alone."

"Okay, two singles, then," Theo declared.

Instead of inner tubes shaped like the world's biggest and most inedible doughnuts, the woman slid over two odd-shaped foam rafts. They were long, with a flat bottom and raised walls along the sides. They were also

40

brown and looked like nothing so much as an open coffin.

"If you're going on the slides, lie flat and cross your arms over your chest," she said. "Or you can clasp your hands together over your stomach in peaceful repose. And don't go on any slides without a lifeguard posted!" The last part was delivered in a whispered hush, with the attendant looking around as though afraid of getting caught delivering a perfectly reasonable warning.

Theo shoved Alexander's coffin—no, *raft*, he had to think of them as rafts or he would never get in—at him, took hers, and took off at what was as close to running as she could possibly manage without actually running.

Alexander followed her. Rafts. Rafts were also made of wood and were rectangular. Though they weren't usually peaked at the top like a roof that got cut off flat. No, that shape was reserved for coffins.

"Rafts," he muttered to himself.

"You saw a rat?" Theo called over her shoulder, not breaking stride. Her only issue with the rafts was that she didn't feel like they were the most aerodynamic shape. They might create drag, slowing down her times.

"At this point, rats wouldn't surprise me," Alexander answered. They arrived at the looming tower and went up the stairs, winding around and around. The wind sang through the gaps between the steps, a mournful sound, and Alexander could hear gulls crying somewhere nearby.

Not gulls. There were no gulls here. But *something* was crying. Before he could place it, they were at the first slide. A leering gargoyle mouth enclosed it, water gushing forth from its pursed, garish lips. But there was a brass chain across the entrance, blocking their way.

"Have you started looking yet?" a lifeguard asked. She was young, with hair as pale as the underside of a toad and eyes to match. Instead of a red swimsuit, she wore an old-timey bathing suit. It was black and white striped, and it went down to her knees. She was holding a parasol over her head. Overall, she gave the impression of transparency. Like if the sun hit her just right, you could see right through her. Which was probably why she had the parasol.

"Looking for what?" Alexander responded.

"What was lost."

"What was lost? Is it a scavenger hunt?" Alexander felt a thrill of excitement. Aunt Saffronia had said something about finding what was lost, too. Alexander loved scavenger hunts—in fact, one of the highlights of every summer was an epic scavenger hunt his parents put together. Sometimes it was around their neighborhood, sometimes part of a trip. Theo loved it, too. Even Wil would participate ... by using Rodrigo to look things up and solve clues, of course.

"There are always scavengers." The lifeguard looked out over the park, sighing mournfully, but offered no further details, much to Alexander's annoyance.

"Um, can I go down the slide now?" Theo asked. She didn't want to think about the summer scavenger hunt they were missing out on this year. It made the bees flare up again. Besides, they were wasting precious slide time.

The lifeguard shrugged. "While in life, agency is your own."

Taking this as permission, Theo unhooked the brass chain. "How should I go down?" she asked, already bouncing with excitement.

"Lie all the way back, clasp your hands, and enjoy oblivion."

Alexander stepped in front of Theo. "Oblivion? Like ... being unconscious? Or destroyed?"

The lifeguard blinked her unnerving eyes. "Oblivion is the name of the slide."

"Metal." Theo nudged Alexander out of the way, slapped her raft down, and climbed in.

"Release yourself to sweet oblivion," the lifeguard said. Then a gush of water from the gargoyle's mouth pushed Theo down.

And it

was

AWESOME.

Theo laughed at every plunge. Her raft took the corners wildly, nearly flying off the slide. At one point, she entered a tunnel so dark she didn't know whether her eyes were open. The bottom ejected her with such force that she skipped along the exit pool like a rock across a pond, finally tipping out near the stairs.

Whatever else this park was, its slides were the *best* she had ever been on. A single week might not be enough time to get tired of them, assuming the rest were like this. And the biggest bonus? All she could feel was exhilaration—a feeling she was happy with because she understood it.

After a minute, Alexander shot out, too. He was wide-eyed, speechless as he splashed free of the pool, dragging his raft.

"That was—" he said.

"Awesome?" Theo suggested.

"That was—"

"Incredible?"

"That was—"

"The best slide you've ever been on in your entire life?"

"That was ... scary."

"I know!" Theo cackled, racing back to the tower. There were six other slides to try, and she was hopeful they were each as awesome, incredible, best-slide-ever, and also scary but in a good way. But Alexander dragged his feet. At the bottom of the tower, he couldn't quite manage to set foot on the stairs.

"What's the holdup?" Theo demanded.

"I think I'll take a break from the slides."

"After only one?"

One had been enough for him. The unexpected push from the rush of gargoyle water had been bad, and it had only gotten worse. Even though the tunnel section was short, he couldn't stop thinking about getting stuck in it, water rushing over him, no way out. Obviously there had been a way out—and it had been a fast way out!—but it didn't stop his brain from imagining other scenarios. "Why don't I time you going down them?"

"Do you have a watch?"

Alexander did not. But he also did not want to go on any more terrifying slides. He wished he could do the scavenger hunt, but the lifeguard hadn't given him any details. "Wave to me when you start and I'll count."

"Fine," Theo grumbled. She was disappointed, but when Alexander decided not to do something, it was almost impossible to make him. She had learned that the hard way. Just as Alexander had learned when Theo decided to do something, it was almost impossible to stop her.

Theo went up alone. She wished Alexander was with her, but she was too busy flinging herself into Oblivion, Abandon Hope, Infinite Plunge, Mortal Coil, the Other Side, and the Afterlife to care too much. The best part was, there was hardly anyone else there. She only had to wait a couple of times behind a few shivering teens. One of the trips up the stairs, she crossed paths with a mother leading her pouting child down. "It's just not safe!" the woman complained. "Why aren't there more lifeguards?"

Which was weird, because there were. Or at least, there was *one* lifeguard. The same one they had already met, who seemed to follow Theo diligently from slide to slide. Theo never saw her on the stairs, but somehow she was always waiting at whatever slide Theo picked.

Alexander stayed at the bottom of the tower and dutifully counted Theo's times. Infinite Plunge was the fastest, Mortal Coil the longest, but Theo wanted to time multiple runs down the same slide to see if she could improve. He was really wishing he had brought the parasol. It wasn't sunny, exactly, but sitting on the walkway watching for Theo's signals and then counting until she rocketed into the pool at the bottom did leave him feeling exposed. He kept rubbing the back of his neck and found himself turning around as though expecting someone to be watching him. He never saw anyone, though.

The park was nearly empty, but there were a few unsupervised teens also going down the slides. "I can't believe there aren't any lifeguards!" one said, incredulous but delighted.

Alexander would not be delighted by that. Even the idea worried him. But he was also confused, because he had met the lifeguard. And even Theo wouldn't go on slides without a lifeguard present. Would she?

He double-checked as she came careening out of her seventeenth ride. "There are lifeguards, right?"

"Yes, of course!" she said, breathless as she dragged her raft out of the water and headed immediately back up.

But Alexander wasn't reassured. The relative emptiness of the park wasn't exciting. It was unnerving. At one point a child ran by, crying, followed by her harried father. Alexander looked in the direction they had come from and thought he saw a glimpse of the ticket booth woman, still smiling. But then she was gone. And he had to focus on counting or face Theo's wrath.

"Okay," Theo said, finally worn out. She had done each of the slides three times, and her legs were burning from climbing those endless winding stairs. "Should we check out their lazy river?"

"Yes, please!" That was definitely more Alexander's style. Not the lazy part, but the implied calm. He had seen it from his first and only trip up the tower, so he pointed them in the right direction. After a few bends in the path, an iron sign hung above an ominous gate. *The River Styx*, it declared.

"Oh, Edgar's river. Wasn't the River Styx the entrance to Hades?" Theo asked. Alexander loved mystery and mythology. Theo loved nonfiction, and they traded information they thought the other might like.

"Yup." Alexander really wished they had gone for funny names instead. He didn't want to take a raft on the river to the underworld.

But Alexander was reassured when he saw Edgar from the store standing at the entrance to the river. He had changed from his fancy suit to an old-fashioned swimsuit like the tower lifeguard, but his polished brass name tag was still pinned in place. Next to the fancy engraved letters of his name he had put a smiley face sticker. He smiled like his sticker when he saw them, adjusting his glasses.

"Hello again. You forgot your sun protection." He was holding his own parasol above his head. And Alexander had to admit, it looked kind of cool. Or maybe it was just that Edgar seemed like the type of person who never cared what other people thought of him, and therefore made everything look cool and easy. Edgar held out a ceramic jar. "My aunt makes this all-natural cream." He paused, his brow furrowed in worry. "Or, at least, she used to. Anyway. Smear some of this on your faces and you won't burn."

They dipped two fingers in. The cream was cool and thick, and they laughed at each other's ghostly pallor after applying it.

"You could almost work here," Edgar said. Then he gestured at their bright suits. "Though you're breaking dress code."

Alexander felt a clench of fear until he realized Edgar was joking. He hated breaking any rules, even if it was just dress code.

"Some codes are better off broken," Theo said, laughing. They threw their rafts into the river entrance pool and climbed on. Edgar grabbed a long pole and gently pushed them into the current. It was swifter than they were expecting, but with a mist hovering over the water and numerous caves and overhangs, the rush of the water was pleasant and hypnotic. Every once in a while, they heard the rumor of other voices, but they never saw anyone else. It was hard to say how many loops they had done. The trees were heavy, and the river seemed to curve and twirl and twist in unpredictable ways.

It was the stillest Alexander had ever seen Theo be, lying in her raft, staring up through the trees at the sun. In fact, it was Alexander who broke their reverie when his stomach growled like a forgotten predator lurking in the shadows.

Theo sat up so fast she almost tipped out of her raft. "Me too!" she said, responding to Alexander's stomach. They noticed Edgar up ahead and waved to him. He used his same pole to hook them out of the current and to the shore.

"Can we leave our rafts here?" Theo asked, bouncing from foot to foot in her eagerness.

"Of course," Edgar answered.

She took off, Alexander struggling to catch up. Ahead, there was something that looked like a restaurant. Theo ducked inside. Just before Alexander got to the door, he heard a cry of absolute horror, a bloodcurdling sound of despair.

"Theo!" he shouted, running for the door, terrified of what he would find when he got there.

CHAPTER
FIVE

Theo stood, frozen, staring at the elegant, handwritten menu in front of her.

It was a joke.

It had to be a joke.

She looked up at the tall man with a stately mustache and a dreary suit in front of her. "But . . . none?"

He shook his head.

"Not in the entire park?"

Alexander rushed in behind her, out of breath. "What is it? What happened?"

Theo turned, devastated. She almost couldn't

form the words. They came out a tortured whisper. *"There are no churros here."*

"I do not know what a churro is," the man said, apologetic. His name tag read *Robert*, but there was no smiley-face sticker. "But we have a lovely afternoon tea service. You will, however, have to follow the dress code. If you do not have something appropriate, we can provide it for you."

"Is there—" Alexander scrambled for words, trying to fix this for Theo. "Is there somewhere else to eat? Somewhere more casual? With, like, burgers and fries? And churros?"

"You will find none of those in the park," Robert said, at last growing exacerbated. "I pride myself on our menus, and I will not sully the great reputation of this noble institution with . . ." His nose wrinkled in distaste. ". . . french fries or any other nationality of fries whatsoever. If you would like to join us for afternoon tea, please go and change. You both may choose whether to wear dresses or trousers, so long as your look is neat and clean. And no bare feet!" He turned and walked behind a heavy velvet curtain.

Alexander put a comforting hand on Theo's shoulder.

"Come on. Let's go find Wil. We need the credit card if we're going to get food anyway. And maybe there's another option."

Theo's good mood had evaporated faster than a wet footprint on cement in the sunshine. She trudged back to their cabasoleum to find Wil laid out on a towel, looking at Rodrigo. "Where are you?" she whispered to the screen.

"Right here?" Theo answered.

"Not you," Wil said. "How's it going." It wasn't really a question, though, and she didn't seem to care about the answer.

"Alexander was arrested for graffitiing the tower. We need the credit card to bail him out." Theo held out her hand.

"Hmm?" Wil said.

"Credit card."

Wil handed it over without question.

"Should we change into our normal clothes?" Alexander asked.

"We'll be too wet. Nothing is worse than wet jeans."

Alexander could list ten things worse than wet jeans just off the top of his head, including having to go down Oblivion again, but he didn't want to argue with Theo when she was already in a terrible no-churros mood.

"Wil, did Edgar tell you any other places to eat here?"

At Edgar's name, Wil's head snapped up, eyes suddenly focused. "Edgar?" She looked around as though saying his name might summon him.

"He's not here. We were just wondering if there's anywhere else to eat in the park besides the one restaurant."

"No, I think there's just one." With no Edgar in sight, Wil went back to her phone.

"Do you want to come get lunch with us?" Alexander asked.

"Afternoon tea, you mean," Theo said, sticking out her tongue.

"No, not the tongue, young lady," Alexander said in his best extremely British voice. "One must stick out their *pinkie* for afternoon tea." Theo cracked and smiled.

"Busy," Wil said. "I'll get something later."

Theo and Alexander didn't see how Wil was any more or less busy than she normally was, or why she couldn't eat while tapping on her phone, which is what she always did—they had once watched her eat an entire enchilada without spilling a single drop while never once looking at her plate, which they agreed should be added to the next Olympics, but they never could decide whether winter or summer would be the better venue for it.

They toweled off as best they could, left the towels in the sun to dry, and hurried back to the restaurant. The same stately mustachioed gentleman greeted them.

"Are you here for afternoon tea?"

"Yes," Theo said through her teeth, scowling.

"Thank you," Alexander added.

"And I see you will be needing outfits. Would you prefer dresses or trousers?"

Theo requested a dress. She liked the freedom of having her legs bare, and one could actually run quite quickly in a dress without the stiff structure of jeans. Alexander requested trousers. They sounded much fancier than pants, and he was strangely excited to see what afternoon tea was, with or without churros.

Robert escorted them to changing rooms. They struggled into the offered clothes, stepped out, and burst into laughter at the sight of each other.

"You look like a depressed Christmas present," Alexander said, taking in the stiff black satin of Theo's dress, complete with an elaborate ruffled bow at her neck.

"All the other dresses were white. It'd be like wearing curtains. Meanwhile, *you* look like someone harvested the butler crop too soon and you weren't quite ripe." Theo had a point. Alexander was wearing a suit that looked like a tuxedo. All he needed was a towel to put over one arm, and he could have been a background player in his mother's favorite show.

"Shall we?" he said, holding out his elbow and bowing.

Instead of taking his elbow, Theo offered one of her own, elbowing him in the stomach and laughing. "Come on, nerd. Let's get this tea time over with. Oblivion is calling my name."

Robert met them at the front of the restaurant. He nodded at their outfits, pleased with the results in spite of their wet hair and sandaled feet, and then led them back behind the curtain. Once again, nothing was what they had expected from a water park restaurant.

There was a crystal chandelier scattering rainbow-prism light through the room. Heavy drapes made every corner seem dim and mysterious. Several tables were set with delicately patterned blue-and-white china, and more forks, knives, and spoons than Theo or Alexander knew what to do with. They suspected someone had gotten confused and just dumped out half the silverware drawer next to each plate. Each table had a creamy lace tablecloth that definitely could not be drawn on with crayons, and the chairs were heavy wood with velvet cushions. A couple of the tables had families already at them, with kids pulling at the necks of their borrowed clothes and parents giggling at the formality of it, taking photos of their children. Theo wished her parents were here to laugh with. And then she was buzzing again, thinking about how her parents weren't here, which reminded her of all the things she was mad about, including the absence of churros. There were just certain foods that went with certain places. A water park without churros was surely violating some sort of law.

Robert pulled out their chairs and then placed cloth napkins in their laps. "You will find the tea service schedule next to your plate. There are no substitutions. There are no—"

"Coke?" Theo asked.

"What?"

"Can I get a Coke?"

"This is afternoon tea. Not afternoon soda." He scowled, tugging at his fine mustache.

"But you have to have Coke."

"We do not, and I resent anyone who thinks we should. Your server will be out shortly." The gentleman turned and elegantly stomped into the back.

Edgar sat at their table. "Hello!" he said, adjusting his glasses. "Is Wil with you?"

"No," Theo said. "She's busy with Rodrigo."

Edgar's face fell. "Rodrigo? Is he her . . . your . . . ?"

"Not *he*," Alexander said. "It. Rodrigo is her phone."

"Oh!" Edgar brightened, straightening his vest. "Well, I'm glad you two are here, at least. I don't normally come to afternoon tea, but it's a special one. It's my aunt's birthday."

"Will there be cake?" Theo asked hopefully. First no churros and now no Coke. She needed sugar, and she needed it soon.

"Oh, yes! My aunt loves cake. Last year she had a three-tier spun-sugar marvel. My dads ate half of it by themselves." A sad expression drifted over his face as he looked at the empty chairs next to himself.

"Was it like the one on season seventeen of *The Magnificent English Confectionary Challenge?*" Alexander asked excitedly. It was his favorite show. Not only did it showcase baked goods he rarely had any desire to eat, but they always adhered to the strictest food-safety protocols, which was deeply soothing to watch.

Theo only liked it when cakes fell over or someone said things like "Oh, great fiddling cat innards!" instead of regular boring American sayings like "Oh, swear word." But she very much liked the sound of a three-tiered sugar cake. Maybe it would even taste almost like a churro.

Alexander looked around. Other than Edgar, there were only a couple of families and one table of teens with heavy eyeliner and a vast assortment of piercings between them. Given that there weren't any other restaurants or food stands, it seemed strange that more people weren't here.

"Is the park usually this empty?" Alexander asked. Maybe it got more crowded in the afternoons, when it was warmest.

Edgar lowered his eyes so they were hidden behind the reflection off his glasses. "Oh, um. Well. You see, lately—"

He was cut off by several people swooping through the curtain and into the room. One of them was Wil. She had apparently decided to join them. She took the chair next to Edgar, flashing him a smile before looking back down at her phone. Somehow *her* restaurant-provided dress looked cool, more like she was going to marry and/ or fight an ancient vampire count than like she was molding underneath a dry Christmas tree, like Theo's.

Behind Wil came several of the employees they had

already met. The tower lifeguard—who Theo now realized was not one very industrious lifeguard who had been at every slide but actually seven nearly identical girls. Theo waved to them, and they waved in unison, drifting to the tables in the back of the room and sitting together. No one else acknowledged them.

"Where did they come from, a copy machine?" Alexander whispered to Theo.

"No, silly. Obviously a 3D printer, but one that ran out of colors."

They both hid their giggles behind their hands as the turkey-vulture man, the raft-booth woman, and the restaurant gentleman came in. Alexander was glad that at least a few other guests were there; otherwise he would have worried they were crashing a private birthday event.

Theo didn't worry about that, because she was too busy wondering what kind of cake was going to come out and how many pieces she would be allowed to have.

A woman swept into the room. Literally swept, her dress so long it dragged on the floor, conveniently picking up any stray dust or crumbs. The dress was the color of a bruise. Not a cool new one, but an old one, somewhere between gray and yellow and purple and brown all at once. It went from the floor to the top of her neck and buttoned so tightly around her wrists Theo fidgeted just looking at it.

"Good afternoon," she said, not taking off her green glasses. It was the woman from the ticket booth.

"Good afternoon, Mrs. Widow," the employees all intoned in unison.

Her meandering eyebrows twitched. "We have guests." She was not pleased about it. Her voice sounded like detention felt. Or at least how Alexander imagined detention felt; he had never actually received detention. Theo had, once, for scaling the side of the school building. Her argument that they shouldn't have used such climbable bricks if they didn't want kids to climb it didn't seem to sway the principal. But for detention she had been assigned to help clean the gym, which she actually enjoyed, because the gym teacher had been impressed by her climbing and let her shimmy to the roof rafters and remove old birds' nests and the odd thrown shoe.

However, Mrs. Widow's voice did not sound like exciting detention. It sounded like a windowless room, with no doors and no clocks and no way out.

"It is our birthday," she said.

Alexander looked around to see who else's birthday it was, but no one stood or anything.

"I have instructed the cook to make my favorite dessert." She gestured, and the melted-candle woman wheeled out what was definitely *not* a spun-sugar, three-tiered cake. It looked like an extremely large pie.

"I give you," the chef said, in the saddest voice Theo had ever heard, "a . . . traditional Victorian mince pie."

"Oh no," Alexander whispered.

"What?" Theo asked. "Pie is all right, I guess. As long as it comes with ice cream." Clearly Theo had not been paying enough attention to *The Magnificent English Confectionary Challenge.*

"No. It's from the *Victorian* era," Alexander said. Which, if Theo had been paying attention, she would have known was a very, very bad sign already. She just nodded as though that information meant nothing. Alexander took a deep breath, steeling himself, and continued. "It has sugar."

Theo nodded. Pies should have sugar.

"And it has raisins."

Theo squinched her face in a frown. In an ideal world, nothing would have raisins, except maybe toddlers who didn't know that raisins were grapes without souls. Anyone who put raisins into cookies or baked goods was just someone who hated joy. But maybe it could still be good.

"And it has . . . meat."

"Wait, what?" Theo sat back in outrage. "A pie with sugar and raisins and meat? What is wrong with these people?"

Edgar also looked aghast. "She always has her special cake. I don't understand."

"Maybe the food will be good?" Alexander offered, hopeful.

"And for the main courses, we have—" The chef seemed to be in a fight with her own tongue, trying to say the words but unwilling to. Finally, she shuddered, then blurted out, "*Jellied eel and pickled oysters good day.*" She turned on her heel and stomped out of the room.

Alexander wanted to cry. Theo wanted to break something. Wil hadn't been listening at all. There were horrified-sounding murmurs from somewhere in the room. The families with younger kids stood and hurried out. The teen table whispered in outrage to each other. "I've been coming here for four years," one teen with fantastically bold cat-eye eyeliner said, "and this is *not* how it usually is."

Edgar leaned close to Theo and Alexander. "I don't know what's going on here, but save yourselves. Take this key. The third armoire on the left has my personal snack stash. Don't tell anyone, and don't let them see you eating it." He slipped a key into Alexander's hand under the table.

"Thank you," Alexander said, and he meant it. Whatever was going on here, he didn't want to taste any of it. "Are you coming, Wil?" he whispered.

Wil didn't look up, waving a hand. "I'm good."

"But—"

Theo grabbed Alexander's hand. "We can't save her if she doesn't want to be saved. Let's go!"

They stood up. Everyone in the room looked at them. "S-sorry," Alexander stuttered, panicking at being the center of attention. "I just remembered that my, uh, shoes are much too comfortable to match this suit."

"Ah," the employees said, nodding in unison. Alexander and Theo rushed out and into the fresh air. They hadn't taken off their restaurant clothes, but Theo wasn't going back in there for anything. The specter of mince pie haunted her steps as she ran toward Edgar's shop.

"Meat!" she cried.

"It doesn't usually have meat anymore. Just spices. But

if they're going traditional, it will." Alexander shuddered again, just thinking about it.

"Even if there's no meat, a pie with *raisins?* Why would anyone do that to pie? It's criminal! It's an outrage!"

"It's worse than your dress."

Theo spun dramatically. "It is! Which shouldn't even be possible!" She flicked the heavy bow around her neck. "Do you think we can leave these clothes in the shop for Edgar?"

Alexander didn't want to, just in case it wasn't allowed. But he really didn't want to go back to the restaurant. He was terrified that if he set foot in there, the jellied eels would come for him, all wobbling and eelish. He didn't know what a jellied eel tasted like, and vowed he would never find out.

"I can't imagine Edgar getting mad at us." Which was saying something, because Alexander was very good at imagining people getting mad at him, even though it very rarely happened. They entered the empty shop, took off their restaurant clothes—only slightly damp from the swimsuits they still wore underneath—and found the snack armoire.

"Edgar is my new best friend," Theo said, staring at the treasure trove Edgar had bequeathed them.

"Mine, too," Alexander agreed. They pulled out a bag of potato chips, two granola bars—with chocolate chips, not raisins, because Edgar was not a monster—and a couple cans of soda. The soda was room temperature and off-brand, but compared to jellied eels and sugared meat pie, it was the best thing they had ever tasted.

They had just finished snacking their fill when Edgar and Wil came in. Wil seemed surprised to see them. She was generally surprised by anything that wasn't her phone screen.

"Hey, twerps," she said. "Weren't you in the restaurant?" She looked behind herself as though expecting them to also be following her.

"We left like an hour ago," Theo said.

"Thanks to Edgar," Alexander added.

"Oh," Wil said with a shrug, going back to Rodrigo.

"How was the food?" Alexander asked, morbidly curious.

Wil shrugged. "I dunno. Cold. I wasn't really paying attention."

"Was the mince pie . . . traditional?"

Edgar gave them a tight smile. "Dreadfully traditional, I'm afraid. I *am* sorry about that. I don't understand. Every year since I can remember, we've had a giant cake for my aunt's birthday. And now she says her favorite is Victorian mince pie?" He shook his head.

"Mrs. Widow is your aunt?" Alexander asked, offering Edgar a bag of chips.

Edgar took it, absentmindedly eating a few. "Yes. Nearly every employee in the park is related. If they aren't, they've worked here for so long they're basically family. I've worked summers here since I was old enough to blow a whistle. But things have been different ever since . . ." He trailed off.

"Ever since what?" Theo prodded.

"Well, ever since we lost my uncle to the Cold, Unknowable Sea."

"Was he a sailor?" Alexander asked.

"Is that why your aunt is Mrs. Widow now?" Theo added.

Edgar shook his head. "No, her last name is Widow."

"That's unfortunate foreshadowing," Wil said, not looking up.

"And my uncle wasn't a sailor. He was the co-manager of the water park. They've run it together for decades."

"If he wasn't a sailor, how did he get lost at sea? Was it a cruise?" Alexander was terrified of cruises and not just because so much of the food was done buffet style, which he had genuine concerns about as far as contamination and proper temperature maintenance went. Even besides the food, being trapped in a giant, floating hotel with thousands of strangers sounded like a nightmare to him.

"No, sorry, I mean we lost him in *our* Cold, Unknowable Sea. The wave pool."

"The wave pool?" Theo looked horrified. "He drowned in the wave pool right next to our cabasoleum?"

"Caba-what? But no, he didn't drown. He disappeared. We lost him, as in, no one knows where he went. He ran across the park, swam into the Cold, Unknowable Sea, and then just . . . never came out. But my aunt is in the process of having him legally declared dead. Maybe that's why she's acting so odd."

Alexander and Theo shared a worried look. No wonder the park was almost empty, if people were disappearing.

"Don't run," Theo whispered.

"That's how people disappear," Alexander answered back.

What kind of water park was this?

CHAPTER
SIX

That evening, back in Aunt Saffronia's kitchen, Theo and Alexander were both relieved to see groceries had appeared in the cupboards and the fridge. It was an odd assortment—some of it had weird packaging, like it came from another decade—but as far as Alexander could tell, it was safe. No churros, though. But it wouldn't have mattered. Churros were meant to be consumed outside, the hot sun warming your shoulders, the cinnamon and sugar coating your fingers with sticky delight.

Theo had still enjoyed the slides after lunch, and the lazy river had still been dreamy, but it had been more difficult to really enjoy the park with the Cold, Unknowable Sea crashing against the rocks next to their cabasoleum. Alexander couldn't stop staring at it, wondering how someone could be *lost* there. And Theo couldn't figure it out, either, which annoyed her to no end.

At least the park closed promptly at five. Theo wouldn't admit it, but she didn't want to be anywhere near that hungry cave mouth after dark. Alexander felt the same way, and he would definitely admit it.

And he *did* admit it. "I don't want to be anywhere near that hungry cave mouth after dark."

"Someone is still hungry?" Aunt Saffronia wrung her hands, staring at a point above their heads. "But there is food now. I thought . . . I thought you would be satisfied by food. What else do you eat?" Her odd, vague eyes widened, and she almost looked right at them.

"No, no," Alexander said, feeling bad that he'd made her worry. "This is good. We're good. We're talking about one of the attractions at Fathoms of Fun."

"Oh, what did you find?" Her gaze—still focused on some distant point they couldn't see—sharpened, and in a way it was almost like they could see her more clearly, too.

"It was weird," Alexander said.

"Kind of fun, definitely weird," Theo agreed.

"Cute," Wil said. Which was weird, because there was definitely nothing cute about the downright gloomy design of the park, or the food, or really anything Theo and Alexander could think of. "He was—I mean, it was really nice."

Theo and Alexander latched on with sudden awareness. Wil had stayed behind in the shop. She only came to lunch when Edgar did, and she was willing to eat raisin-and-meat pie and jellied eels just to hang out with him.

"Wil—" Theo gasped.

"Is—" Alexander exclaimed.

"In—" Theo continued.

"No mood for you two to comment on any aspect of my private life, thank you very much." Wil didn't look up, but she didn't need to. Her tone of voice was enough to get them to shut their mouths. It was a tone that said *I'm about to take my eyes off my phone and you really, really don't want me to, because I control Mom and Dad's credit card and therefore your happiness for this entire summer.*

"But what did you find?" Aunt Saffronia asked. She sounded intense.

Alexander frowned. "We told you what we thought of the park."

"That's not what I'm asking. I'm asking what have you found? Have you been looking? You should look closer. You need to look closer. We all need you to look closer. We need *time*." Then she blinked, smiled distractedly, and drifted out of the room.

Alexander, puzzled by Aunt Saffronia's intensity, tugged on the heavy brass locket around his neck. He had tried to take it off when they left the park, but it wouldn't come undone. Wil was still wearing hers, too. Theo, however, had hers on the table.

"Why won't mine come off?" Alexander asked.

"Maybe it's supposed to stay on the whole week, since that's the package we picked?" Theo said. "Like a wristband so you have in and out privileges."

"Then why did yours come off?"

Theo shrugged. "Never clasped right. Let's have a race to see who can eat the most ice cream before getting brain freeze." She had missed out on churros and cake today and was determined to make up for it.

"Are we really going back there every day for the rest of the week?" Alexander asked, his stomach feeling uneasy even before he ate too much ice cream.

"What else are we going to do? Aunt Saffronia doesn't have a television, or books, or—"

"Wi-Fi," Wil said.

"Or Wi-Fi. The park was pretty fun today. We'll just be sure to pack our own food tomorrow."

"And stay out of the wave pool."

Theo nodded, in full agreement. They would stay out of the wave pool, no matter what.

"Lost!" Alexander exclaimed. "It *is* a scavenger hunt!"

"Huh?" Theo responded. Wil didn't look up, but Alexander grabbed Theo's arm and pulled her away to speak privately anyhow.

"Aunt Saffronia told us to look for what was lost. And the lifeguard said the same thing. And then when Edgar was talking about Mr. Widow, he didn't say he was missing or dead—he said he was *lost*. Theo, I think—I think we're supposed to find Mr. Widow!"

CHAPTER
SEVEN

"But why send us on a scavenger hunt without any clues?" Theo asked as they got ready in their cabasoleum the next morning.

"Maybe the lack of clues is part of the fun?" Alexander said.

"You haven't been having much fun." Theo didn't say it meanly. It was the truth.

"Yeah." And it seemed weird that their parents would put together such an elaborate setup just to do their annual scavenger hunt. Weird, and a little mean. And while the Sinister-Winterbottom parents were definitely weird, they were never mean. Maybe Aunt Saffronia was trying to do a hunt in their absence? She hadn't answered any questions on the way here this morning. But Alexander and Theo were beginning to figure out she just didn't *hear* questions unless she wanted to.

Theo, ready to go, shrugged. "Keep an eye out for clues or whatever." She had to keep moving to outpace the bees that seemed to be building an entire hive in her chest now.

But Alexander found it was impossible to look for clues while sitting under his parasol, counting slide times for Theo. Alexander wanted to go to the lazy river or try to interview some of the employees, but at least Theo wasn't pressuring him to do the slides again. He wasn't ready. He might never be ready.

When it was lunchtime, Theo slapped her forehead. "I left my towel at Aunt Saffronia's. I'll go grab another one. Meet you at the cabasoleum." She speed-walked alone to the shop. The door was unlocked, but Edgar wasn't there. The extra towel from the day before was still on the table, so she grabbed it.

Back at the cabasoleum, Alexander was wrapped in his own towel and glaring at the wave pool, deep in thought. Or *trying* to be deep in thought but not really coming up with anything besides the clues he already had: Aunt

Saffronia said they needed time and to find what was lost. The lifeguard had also told them to find what was lost. And Edgar had said Mr. Widow had been lost in the Cold, Unknowable Sea. Maybe it was a scavenger hunt, or maybe it was serious. Either way, he wanted to solve it.

Theo dried her hair so she looked like a cactus, then laid her towel out in the sun instead of crumpling it on the ground out of respect for whatever Edgar felt for it. She'd return it tomorrow when she remembered her other one.

"Weird," Theo said, looking at it all laid out. "They even printed the towels to look like rock walls."

"They do love a theme here," Alexander agreed. "But only your towel is printed like rocks. The others just have a pattern like wallpaper."

"Not just rocks. Look, that rock has a star on it." Theo pointed. Sure enough, one of the rocks on the rock-patterned towel had a faint star. "A lot of effort for towels. Do you want to head to the restaurant?"

Alexander's stomach lurched in horror, but then Theo laughed. "Just kidding. I packed us lunches. Let's go eat in Edgar's shop. He wasn't there yet, but maybe he'll come. Anyway, I like it better than our mausoleum."

Alexander didn't disagree. Plus, he wanted to interview

Edgar, to see if there were any other clues the nice young man could offer. This time, Edgar was there. He opened the door to the shop with a smile that faded slightly as he looked toward the restaurant.

"Are you going to eat there?" Alexander tried not to shudder. He felt very bad for Edgar indeed, having to eat there again after what he endured yesterday.

"Robert, the host, didn't come in today, so they're not seating anyone."

As if on cue, a teenage couple walked past, scowling. "No food in the whole park? This is ridiculous. It wasn't like this last summer," one of the girls said.

The other girl shrugged. "Let's just go. This isn't really fun anymore."

Maybe Edgar's expression was less worry about the menu and more worry about the restaurant being closed, which meant there was no food for sale in the park. Now that Alexander thought about it, he had only seen two other families the whole time he'd been watching the slides. So it didn't really matter if the restaurant wasn't seating anybody, since there were so few bodies to seat.

"That's okay. We packed our lunches. We can share." Theo waved her brown bag.

"And I have my snack trove," Edgar said. "We'll break into it again."

As they sat in a circle on the floor—the couches looked too fancy to eat on, and even though Edgar's suit was too nice for the floor, he didn't seem to mind—Alexander chewed on a sandwich and also a thought. "So if an employee doesn't show up, they just . . . don't open the one restaurant in the park?"

"He's never not shown up before." Edgar frowned. "Did that make sense? Never . . . not . . . well, what I mean is, this is the first time it's happened. And Jeremiah, our head of park security, didn't come in today, either."

"That's . . . mysterious," Alexander said, seeing how Edgar reacted. But Edgar just looked worried.

"Which one's he? The one with the—" Theo jutted her head out as turkey-vulturey as she could, then formed her fingers into claws and rasped, "No running! That's how you disappear!"

Edgar laughed, then politely tried to cover it with a cough. "Yes, that's Jeremiah. He comes across as intense, but he blames himself for Mr. Widow's disappearance. He takes safety very seriously."

"I appreciate that," Alexander said. "Speaking of Mr.

Widow's disappearance, I don't suppose you have any . . . clues?" His heart raced, hoping that maybe, just maybe, Edgar would wink and smile and produce a handwritten code that they'd have to solve.

No such luck. Edgar shook his head sadly. "Only what I told you. Believe me, we've all tried to figure out what happened to him."

A mystery, then. Not as fun as a scavenger hunt, but more important. Alexander nodded resolutely, determined to get to the bottom of it regardless of whether there was a prize waiting at the end.

But thinking about the bottom and getting to it made him think of the Cold, Unknowable Sea and how he very much didn't want to see the bottom of that.

"What is he like? Mr. Widow, I mean?"

"My uncle is the kindest, gentlest man I've ever known." Edgar smiled. Alexander noticed how Edgar was using present tense instead of past tense, which meant Edgar still believed—or at least wanted to believe— that Mr. Widow was only missing, not dead. "I've spent every summer here for as long as I can remember, and I've always had the best summers. It was a Black-Widow tradition."

"Black widows?" Alexander asked, alarmed as he wondered what was lurking underneath the furniture in their cabasoleum, or even under these couches, or in the dark corners. . . .

"No, sorry, that's my last name. It's hyphenated."

"At least it's shorter than Sinister-Winterbottom," Theo said with a shrug. She still resented how long it took to write out.

"Why is Mrs. Widow having him declared dead?" Alexander immediately regretted asking; it wasn't a very polite question. But he wasn't sure what the etiquette was when someone's uncle was missing but not dead but maybe dead.

"I don't know." Edgar picked at the crust of his sandwich, his frown deepening. "It doesn't make any sense. Nothing she's done lately does. She barely looked for him. And this park is their whole lives, but ever since he went missing, it's like . . ."

"Like what?" Alexander prodded.

"Like she wants it to fail."

"Maybe it makes her sad, because she misses Mr. Widow?"

"Could be." Edgar shrugged. He looked so genuinely

sad and miserable, Alexander decided to stop asking questions for now.

"Maybe we could get Wil's phone to use for a timer," Theo said, industriously scarfing her sandwich and unaware that Alexander was trying to sniff out clues to a mystery. "No offense, Alexander, but I suspect there are some flaws to your sitting-there-and-counting-out-loud method."

"Not as many flaws as there are to your plan to get Rodrigo away from Wil."

"You need a timer?" Edgar asked.

Theo nodded. "I'm trying to time my slide runs and figure out how to go even faster." She hoped Edgar wouldn't tease her. She couldn't explain why it was important to her, only that it was. It felt like if she could focus on that, if she could make this week the most fun ever, she wouldn't miss their parents. The bees would stay quiet in their new hive, where she could ignore them.

"Well then! I have something for you." Edgar went to one of the bell jars and pulled out an old-timey-looking stopwatch. It was encased in brass, with a glass face and a button at the top that started the second hand.

It was also on a chain so Theo could wear it around her neck, much like the entrance locket that wouldn't stay fastened.

"No way!" Theo exclaimed.

"No way," Alexander agreed. He'd be terrified of breaking it. He was already terrified of breaking it just by looking at it.

Edgar smiled and handed it to Theo. "It's a family heirloom, but we never use it. Waterproof." He tapped on the glass face.

"Wow! Thank you!" Theo gasped with joy, taking the stopwatch. As soon as she had laid eyes on it, she had the strangest feeling that it was *meant* to be hers. "It's exactly what I need."

Alexander, still slightly worried about somehow breaking it, was at least relieved that he could stop counting aloud to himself now. He preferred counting to going down the slides, but that didn't mean it wasn't annoying.

The door chimed, and Wil sauntered in, eyes on her phone. "Oh, hey," she said, her voice casual, as though it was surprising to find Edgar exactly where he was supposed to be.

Alexander and Theo had no desire to see what happened when Wil tried to flirt, so they excused themselves. Theo went back to the slides, timer in hand. Alexander sat beneath his parasol, trying to ignore the sound of crashing waves nearby. When Theo tired of the slides—or rather, the stairs to the slides—they let themselves be hypnotized on the lazy river. Every full pass revealed Wil sitting at the guard station next to Edgar, both under the shade of his parasol.

"Oh, Wil," Theo said, pitching her voice low. "I love the way your eyes never look up from your phone."

"Oh, Edgar," Alexander replied, "I also love the way my eyes never look up from my phone." The trees overhead caught their giggles, letting them drape on the branches like moss.

But their giggles caught in their throats as they came around a bend and saw Mrs. Widow, standing on the banks of the river, watching them. In her hand was a long pole with a hook on the end. Without asking permission, she reached out and snagged Alexander's raft. He yelped in surprise. Lightning-quick, Theo grabbed his hand before she could be carried away by the current.

"I hear you've been asking about my husband," Mrs.

Widow said, peering at him from behind those odd green lenses.

"Yes?" Alexander squeaked. "I want to help. Find him, I mean."

"How could *you* find him?" she asked, her lips twisting in a sneer. "I've seen you. You're not even brave enough to go down a waterslide."

"He's really good at finding things!" Theo said, anger flaring at the way Mrs. Widow was trying to make Alexander feel bad. "Our mom loses her keys at least once a day, and he always finds them. Plus he's super smart, and really clever, and anyway, what do you care? Don't you want help?"

"I want you two to mind your own business," she said. "Or else." She gave a sharp push with her pole that sent them spinning away down the river.

When they finally got their rafts under control, Theo glared back toward where they had left Mrs. Widow. "That was messed up."

"Yeah. Why do you think she wouldn't want us looking? Maybe she's worried about our safety."

"Does she strike you as the type to worry about our safety?"

Alexander had to admit she did not.

"You're actually trying to find Mr. Widow?" Theo asked.

"Well, if she doesn't want us to, then maybe—"

"Oh, we're going to find him all right." Theo folded her arms. Mrs. Widow had tried to make Alexander feel bad. If she didn't want them looking for Mr. Widow, then that was *exactly* what Theo was going to do.

CHAPTER

EIGHT

The next morning, as they got ready to leave for the water park, Alexander dug in his suitcase for an extra set of swim trunks. Even though he was upset with his parents, he had to admit the suitcase his mom packed was like magic. Every time he needed something, there it was. So he was surprised to find his fingers brushing a thick envelope. He pulled it out, frowning.

"Did you get a letter?" he asked Theo, who was flopped over the side of her bed, still half-asleep. They shared a room with twin beds covered in lacy blankets. The edges of the room were dark and blurry, the window too far away to bother with opening the curtains.

Theo sat up. "No."

Alexander turned it over in his hands. "It's addressed to all three of us." He carefully slid his finger beneath the seal, opening the envelope, and pulled a creamy card free. He recognized his mother's handwriting right away. She wrote in the most elegant cursive that he tried to imitate but had a hard time reading, much less writing.

Theo could barely read the cursive at all, but she still leaned in, feeling closer to their mother somehow.

"*My dearest children,*" Alexander said, feeling a surge of hope that this was a scavenger hunt after all. He had just missed the first clue. No wonder nothing made sense!

"Do it in her voice," Theo suggested.

"*My dearest children,*" Alexander repeated in a trilling soprano. Theo giggled, and Alexander continued in his normal voice. "*I am sorry for the turn this summer has taken. Sometimes being Sinister catches up to you.*"

"What does that mean?" Theo interrupted.

"I have no idea." Alexander leaned closer to the letter and continued reading. "*Theo, be brave.*"

"That's weird advice."

Alexander agreed. Theo was always brave. She hardly needed encouragement. If anything, their mother usually urged her to greater caution.

Theo read the next part, struggling through the loopy letters. *"Alexander, be cautious."* Theo leaned back, squinting. "Did I read that right?"

"Yeah."

"She's telling you . . . to be cautious. Does she *know* you? Your first words were 'Be careful!'" It was true. Theo's first word was "Go!" Wil's first word was actually a complete sentence, asking her parents to please change the radio station in the car.

"Maybe she got our names mixed up?" Alexander didn't really see how that could have happened, but he also didn't understand why their mother would tell them to be exactly what they already were as though that was useful instruction. This didn't feel at all like a scavenger hunt clue. He read the next sentence. *"And, Wil, use your phone."*

Theo threw her hands up in exasperation. "She's telling Wil to use Rodrigo?! She might as well have told us to breathe. Or told my hair to stand up on end. Or told you to worry about safe food preparation. This is the weirdest letter ever. There has to be something else."

89

"Only this: '*Depend on each other as we are depending on you. Gather the tools. And listen to Saffronia except when you shouldn't. All our love, Mom and Dad.*'"

Alexander had expected to feel better after reading a letter from his mom, but it made him feel even worse. There were no hints, no indication that they were on some elaborate scavenger hunt. And, worse, there was something . . . sinister about the whole thing. And not capital-S Sinister. Just the regular kind, which made his stomach twist with fear that something was going on he didn't know about. Something that took his parents away for the whole summer.

"I thought they'd at least explain," Theo said, her brow like a storm descending over her eyes. Her chest felt like someone had kicked the hive. And added ants, too, so now she was buzzing *and* itching, full to bursting with feelings.

"Explain what?"

"This," Theo said, gesturing at the room around them, but meaning the entire summer around them, devoid of their parents and their home and everything they knew and loved.

Alexander at least felt a little less alone, knowing Theo, too, was upset. "Should we show it to Wil?" he asked.

"And give her even more of an excuse to live inside her phone? If Mom wants her to know that, she can text her." Theo grabbed the letter and threw it back in the suitcase, then slammed it shut. "Come on. We have a Widow to find."

Wil ditched them almost the second they walked into the park. "Gonna go shop," she said, which they knew meant *Gonna go hang out with my phone but also Edgar.*

Theo and Alexander dropped their stuff—which now included several bags of food and snacks, with extra to replace what they had taken from Edgar—at their cabasoleum. Theo glared at the far wall once more. Something wasn't right with it, and she couldn't put her finger on what it was. She was already in a bad mood from their mom's stupid letter and everything felt wrong. She walked to the back of the cabasoleum, putting her hands against the walls.

Alexander was mad, too. But while being mad made Theo twitchy and irritable, it made Alexander feel like he was going to cry. Why did his mom write a letter that didn't give them any answers? It didn't even give them any clues. Just told him to be cautious. Like he wasn't cautious all the time! Like he wasn't worried all the time, and now more than ever thanks to his parents being gone.

Alexander could be brave! He didn't always have to be the cautious one. If Mr. Widow was missing, and he was last seen going into the wave pool, then that's where Alexander would go to look for him. Tugging on his board shorts ties to make sure they weren't loose, he marched right up to the pounding, crashing waves, and jumped in.

And immediately regretted it.

The waves were everywhere, pushing and swirling and tumbling him. He floundered, trying to keep his head above water. He was a strong swimmer—not out of a desire to compete like Theo, but out of a desire to make sure he was always safe around large bodies of liquid—but a particularly rough wave pulled him right through the cave mouth and into the dark interior. It was loud, everything echoing, every wave magnified so they even *sounded* big.

Alexander had never felt so overwhelmed in his life. He certainly wasn't going to find any clues. He could barely find the entrance to the cave, and swimming as hard as he could wasn't making any difference. His breaths started to come faster, panic setting in. Was this what Mr. Widow had felt like? But how had he just disappeared? There was nowhere to go! Alexander would be stuck in this cave forever! His heart pounded so fast it almost drowned out the waves—but then Alexander was thinking of drowning, and forgetting his swim training, and—

Someone shoved a coffin at him. For a terrible moment, Alexander thought this was the end, and they were preparing him for it. But then he realized it was a raft. "Climb on!" a voice echoed.

Alexander grabbed on to the raft, relieved to be free of the waves, even though they still flung him around. At least he was out of the water. He looked up to see Edgar standing there, still in his suit.

"Are you okay?" Edgar shouted.

Alexander nodded. He wasn't, but he didn't want to talk about it. He was shivering, clinging to the raft, and more than a little afraid the motion of the waves was going to make him throw up.

"I've got you." Edgar extended a hook, and Alexander grabbed on. Walking along a narrow ledge lining the pool, Edgar carefully pulled Alexander free, depositing him on the shore, where it was easy to climb out. "You shouldn't be in there without a lifeguard watching you! No one should." Edgar looked back at the wave pool.

"But I wanted to look for—I thought I could find a clue. About Mr. Widow's disappearance." Alexander hung his head, embarrassed.

But Edgar didn't mock him, instead putting a hand on Alexander's shoulder. "That's very kind of you. And very brave! But believe me, I've searched that cave top to bottom."

Alexander glumly nodded. He had *tried* to be brave, and it hadn't done anything except force Edgar to rescue him. "It's impossible, though. There's no other way out. How could he have just disappeared? It's not like he could climb out the roof of the cave, or tunnel under."

"Right. Of course not. That's—" Edgar froze. His eyes went as round as his round glasses. "Excuse me. I must go check on something. Have fun—and stay out of the wave pool!" He hurried away.

"There you are!" Theo said, stepping out of their cabasoleum. She was puzzled to see Alexander already wet. "What happened?"

"I don't want to talk about it," Alexander grumbled.

"Did you go in the wave pool without me?" She was aghast. She hadn't wanted to go in the wave pool. But

Alexander was brave enough to? Her competitive streak flared. Alexander was *never* braver than her.

"It was a mistake," he said, sullenly kicking the puddle forming beneath him.

Annoyed, Theo debated jumping in the wave pool, too, just to prove she could do it. But she didn't want to. So she turned around and looked up at the tower. "Alexander," she hissed, grabbing his arm.

He followed her sight line and frowned. "Is there someone at the top of the tower?"

Just for a moment, they had seen a flash of white and what could have been a person behind one of the windows there.

"Can we get up there?" Theo asked. "How did that person get up there? We could see everything! Maybe find a clue! Maybe there's a lifeguard up there with secret information!"

"We should definitely check it out," Alexander said in unhappy agreement. The top of the tower looked like a lighthouse, but not a cheerful red-and-white lighthouse that one might picnic at to enjoy a view. It looked like a lighthouse that lured ships to rocky coasts to crash and sink, rather than warning them away. It was at least ten stories high, too. He felt dizzy just thinking about it.

On the other hand, though, it was far away from the Cold, Unknowable Sea, which was a definite improvement.

Theo's excitement surged. Alexander had gone in the wave pool without her and hadn't found any clues. She was going to solve it! "What if it's Mr. Widow? And he's hiding up there?"

"Why would he be hiding, though?"

Theo shrugged. The *why* didn't really concern her. She was more interested in *doing* than thinking. "If I were married to Mrs. Widow, I'd hide, too. Come on!" she said, taking off at a walk that was really only a walk in the sense that if someone stopped them she could argue she hadn't been running but really was fast enough to qualify her for most middle school cross-country teams.

They came around a corner and nearly speed-walked into Mrs. Widow. She wore the same fading-bruise dress, and those odd green glasses that hid her eyes.

"Oh," she said, pursing her lips. "You're here again."

"We're going to the room at the top of the tower!" Theo declared, breathless with excitement.

"No, you're not!" Mrs. Widow exclaimed with such force that Alexander took a step back. Then her thin lips peeled themselves into a smile. "I mean, there's nothing there. It's not a real room."

"But we saw someone up there, just now," Alexander said, hating to contradict an adult but knowing what he had seen. He shivered, trying to keep his teeth from chattering. He didn't like being wet, and he especially didn't like being wet from a terrifying wave pool he could still hear in the distance.

"Oh," Mrs. Widow said, her smile getting bigger in the way you sometimes only see part of a spider but then it crawls out of its hole to reveal sinisterly elegant legs and far more body than you ever wanted a spider to have. "It's storage, is all. Someone must be putting something away."

Theo craned her neck to look up at the tower. "You climb up ten flights of twisty, narrow stairs . . . to store things?"

Mrs. Widow's spider smile didn't budge. "Yes," she said. "That's exactly right."

Theo and Alexander shared a look that couldn't help but sweep across the several large buildings all around them that doubtless had far more storage space than a small, round room at the top of a tower.

"Okay," Theo said.

"Run along," Mrs. Widow said.

"We were warned not to run," Alexander said, trying to make it sound like a joke, but Mrs. Widow's meandering eyebrows shot up.

"Who warned you about that?"

"Uh, just . . . one of the employees?" He didn't want to say "a man who looked like a turkey vulture," because it didn't seem nice.

"I see. Well. You have my permission to run. Run all you wish." Mrs. Widow turned and walked away, her skirts trailing on the ground behind her.

"That was—" Alexander started.

"Weird?" Theo suggested.

"Creepy?"

"Irresponsible?"

"A good reason to make sure we don't run at all," Alexander finished. There was something very wrong with Mrs. Widow, and it made him nervous. She didn't act like a grown-up should, much less a grown-up in charge of a potentially hazardous water park.

"Do you think that was true, about storage up in the tower?" Theo asked.

"Why would she lie?"

"I'm not sure. But first she said there wasn't a room

up there, and then she changed her story. Besides, why would she tell us not to look for Mr. Widow? And why would she encourage us to run, when that's how people get hurt?"

"Or disappear," Alexander added. "How about you go on the slides and keep an eye out for a way into the top of the tower?" He knew he should go up and look, but he could feel the tower looming above them, watching, and after being tumbled by the terrible waves, he wanted to stay firmly on the ground.

CHAPTER
NINE

Theo didn't find anything on the slides except water and acceleration. Alexander was almost relieved. As much as he had wanted a mystery to solve, he didn't like Mrs. Widow, and he increasingly didn't like her water park. Maybe they were best off just finishing out the week and then hoping their parents picked them up.

He was cold, and he was sad, and in his attempt to be brave and prove his mother wrong he had only ended up proving to himself that he wasn't brave at all.

After Theo and Alexander had eaten lunch,

they gathered the food to replace Edgar's stash. Wil was lying on a chair, either asleep or looking at Rodrigo. She often slept with it in her hand, so with sunglasses on it was actually impossible to tell whether or not she was awake.

"We're going to pull off a dramatic, high-stakes heist," Theo said.

"I'm the getaway driver. I don't have my license, but stealing nuclear codes is illegal anyway, and two wrongs make a right," Alexander added.

Wil didn't so much as grunt an acknowledgment. Theo and Alexander walked barefooted toward the store where Edgar worked when he wasn't lifeguarding. It seemed like everyone in the park did double duty. Yesterday they had seen the cook-slash-raft-booth-attendant tending to the nearly black roses that lined the walkways, and the day before that the turkey-vulture man slowly but surely sweeping away puddles on the cobblestone paths. They hadn't seen either of them today, though.

They passed a long row of storage lockers. Something about them was weird, but Alexander couldn't put his finger on it. Well, something was weird besides the fact that the lockers weren't brightly painted metal, but rather rich, dark wood, with elaborate scrolling details, and the locks were all angel faces with ornate brass keys inserted into surprised little angel mouths. But it *would* be surprising to have a large key sticking out of your mouth.

Theo, however, noticed what was extra strange right away. "None of the keys are gone," she pointed out. Every cherub mouth was full, which meant every single locker was empty, which meant that no one was using them, which meant there might not be anyone else in the park. It was surprising. But maybe not too surprising, given that the restaurant was still closed and the park owner seemed determined to lurk creepily, getting mad at children and giving dangerous advice. And then there was the utter lack of churros. Theo couldn't really blame people for abandoning Fathoms of Fun.

They were about to open the door to the shop when they heard raised voices. Theo stopped, then leaned closer to the door.

"We shouldn't eavesdrop," Alexander whispered.

"We shouldn't get *caught* eavesdropping," Theo amended, tugging him off the doorstep and into the shadows beneath an ivy-choked awning. The window there was cracked open, so they could hear better.

"—new contracts? I don't understand. Why are you doing this?" It was Edgar. He sounded upset.

The next voice was his aunt Mrs. Widow. "I don't need you to understand. I just need you to sign and make all the other employees do the same. And bring me the old contracts so I can dispose of them. I mean, file them for my records."

"Mr. Widow wouldn't like this."

"Well, he's not here, is he?" Mrs. Widow didn't sound like a woman in mourning. She sounded almost gleefully vicious. But then she paused. "He's not here, is he? Is he? Have you seen him?"

Edgar sounded confused. "No. No one has."

"That's what I thought. I'm leaving the contracts here. Sign yours, and make everyone else sign them, too. Do it, or you'll be sorry."

"Is she threatening him?" Theo whispered.

Alexander shrugged. It sounded like that to him. But Mrs. Widow was Edgar's aunt. Why would she do that?

Then again, Saffronia was their aunt and barely seemed capable of keeping other living beings alive, so maybe being an aunt wasn't something that most people took seriously.

The door next to them burst open, and Theo and Alexander shifted deeper into the shadows as Mrs. Widow swept down the walkway toward the tower.

After waiting long enough that they could reasonably pretend they hadn't overheard the fight, Theo and Alexander went into the shop. Edgar was sitting on the couch, his head in his hands, a stack of paper next to him.

"Hey," Theo said brightly.

"We brought you replacement snacks," Alexander said, his voice gentler. It was clear Edgar was upset. Alexander wondered if they should have just waited and come back later.

Edgar looked up at them and forced a smile. "Thanks! That was really nice of you. I have to go do something. Would you mind stocking the snacks in my armoire?" He undid one key from his large key ring and gave it to Alexander, then walked slowly out, his steps heavier than normal, the papers held away from his body as though he wanted to touch them as little as possible.

"I wonder what that was about?" Alexander asked, unlocking the armoire.

"Mrs. Widow's a bully."

"They talked about Mr. Widow again. She's doing things he wouldn't like." But that just made Alexander feel sad, because he wasn't any closer to finding Mr. Widow. And it looked like, in the meantime, everyone was suffering. He didn't want Edgar to be sad. Edgar was their friend. Not only had he saved Alexander this morning, he had saved them from having to eat jellied eel and mince pie.

What could Alexander do about it if he couldn't even handle a wave pool? Mrs. Widow had been right when she sneered at him in the lazy river. He wasn't brave enough for this.

Theo stuffed the replacement food into the armoire. Even though they had brought more than they took in the first place, there was still plenty of room inside. She kind of wanted to unlock the other armoires and see what else the shop sold, but that would be a betrayal of Edgar's trust. She was tempted to tell Alexander there might be clues, but really, she just wanted to snoop. And Alexander wouldn't approve. She was still sore with him for going into the wave pool without her, and annoyed that her sighting of someone in the tower hadn't magically solved everything. The buzzing inside was *angry*.

"Should we leave the key on the table?" Theo asked.

Alexander stared down at the heavy weight of it in his palm. "Then anyone could take it."

"Which anyones are we worried about?" Theo gestured out the door at the empty park.

"True. Still." Alexander tucked the key under the armoire, behind one of the claw-foot legs. When they talked to Edgar again, he'd tell him where they left it.

His problem was assuming that they would, in fact, talk to Edgar again.

CHAPTER TEN

I f ever there was a day that screamed "Go to a water park!" this was not it. Rather, this day seemed to blearily mumble, "Stay in bed if you know what's good for you." It was overcast and drizzly, with an unseasonably chill wind tangling its fingers through their hair as Aunt Saffronia drove away.

"I can't believe she didn't let us stay home," Alexander grumbled, retreating deeper into his hoodie for warmth. He was still in a bad mood from his tumble in the wave pool yesterday and his lack of progress on the mystery of Mr. Widow.

"You don't have to swim," Wil said, hurrying

past them out of either an eagerness to get into the park or to generate warmth through movement.

"Yes, because there are so many other things to do at a water park," Theo snarled. She hated cold weather, unless she was doing cold-weather things like skiing or snowboarding or snowshoeing or snowball throwing or hot cocoa drinking. And rain was her least favorite weather. There was nothing special that rain made possible, unless you considered looking like a drowned rat to be a fun activity, which Theo did not.

Alexander liked rain but not at a water park. Though he supposed if you were already wet, it wouldn't make a difference to get wetter. It was the principle of the matter, though. You were supposed to *choose* to get wet and then decide when to be dry.

"Go to the library." Wil shrugged, not looking back at them.

They hurried to catch up to her. Alexander paused at the entrance, though. There was someone new in the ticket booth. Instead of Mrs. Widow, there was a glowering man with small, mean eyes and a large, mean mustache. He watched them suspiciously as they walked past.

"We can't go to the library," Alexander said, sharing a confused look with Theo. "We're already at the water park. Aunt Saffronia said we still had things to accomplish here." Those had been her exact words. What did she think they were going to accomplish besides getting rainy raisin skin and avoiding raisin-meat pie?

"You two never look at the maps." Wil slapped her hand against a sheet of parchment pinned to a wrought-iron lamppost. Then she kept walking, face to her phone.

Theo and Alexander peered at the parchment. It was spared from the rain by an overhanging tree. On it was a map of the park. The tower, the sea, the river, the cabanas, the restaurant, the shop, and . . . the library.

"What kind of water park has a library?" Theo asked. Then she shook her head. "Actually, you know what? *This* kind of water park has a library."

"I know I should be surprised, but I'm not really surprised." Alexander was, however, mildly excited. He enjoyed libraries because you could always discover books there you might not otherwise know existed. And also because librarians loved him, and he quite liked being loved. And now he could sit with a good book while Theo went down the slides! Maybe he'd give up entirely on trying to solve Mr. Widow's disappearance. He clearly wasn't brave enough for this sort of thing.

Theo also loved libraries but was generally only

tolerated by librarians. They had all these finicky rules about not climbing the shelves to reach something on the top or even just to see how quickly you could do it. If shelves weren't meant to be climbed, why had they been designed in such a climbable manner?

But books were almost as good as movement. When she got really into a book, all the bees inside went to sleep, because she was feeling the character's feelings instead of her own. And *character's* feelings were always neatly described in orderly letters marching along the page.

"Let's *check it out!*" Theo said, then waited excitedly.

Alexander, predictably, beamed. Theo didn't pun often, but when she did, she knew it would make her brother happy. Both of them were slightly cheered up as they hurried through the rain. They didn't see a single soul on the puddled pathways. But they weren't exactly looking, not even bothering to stop at their cabasoleum to drop their things off. It said a lot about their vacation so far that two twelve-year-olds were excited by the prospect of taking a break in a library instead of swimming.

The library was behind the restaurant, tucked away beneath yawning trees. It was only one story, the stonework even older than the rest of the park, pocked and worn with time. The heavy wooden door swung open with a protesting groan. Inside, it was dim but cozy, light filtering in through an abundance of stained-glass windows. The lamps looked almost like candlelight, warm pools of radiance guiding them. In the center of the library were several old and overstuffed chairs that actually looked cuddly.

"Oh, history!" Theo exclaimed at the same time Alexander said, "Oh, mysteries!" Laughing, they separated to their preferred sections, browsing the shelves. There were no librarians present, and Alexander wasn't sure what the rules were, so he doubted he was allowed to check books out. He very much wanted to. Aunt Saffronia didn't have any books in her house that he'd seen.

Though, now that he tried to picture her house, all he could come up with was the kitchen and their bedroom. Surely there were other rooms. A bathroom, for instance, like the bathrooms at this park. Those all featured full-length, carved wood doors rather than swinging metal doors with far too many inches between the hinges and the walls. The bathrooms here also had fluffy towels instead of paper towels or hand dryers, the toilets had gold chains above that you had to pull to flush them—it had taken Theo way too long to figure that out, standing, staring in absolute befuddlement at the toilet—and the mirrors were all framed with ominous cherubs glaring out from gilded wood.

But try as Alexander might, he could only come up with Saffronia's kitchen and their bedroom.

He turned to Theo to ask her if she remembered Aunt Saffronia's bathroom, but she was already hidden in her section of the library. And when he turned around to the shelves, he forgot what he was wondering about.

This library didn't offer much in the way of new books, but at least it had a variety. Especially in the Gothic and mystery section. He'd had no idea just how many authors named Brontë there were.

Theo, seeing no librarians present, scaled the nearest bookshelf. Just to get a view of the library, she told herself. The tops of the shelves were dusty and unused—except the one right next to her. There was a slender, leather-bound volume there, with a sliding mark cleared through the dust, as though someone had hastily shoved the book up here. She was extremely pleased with herself. If she hadn't industriously climbed the bookshelf, no one would have ever known that book was there!

She quickly climbed her way along the shelves to the book and pulled it free—and sneezed so hard she nearly fell. Her feet slipped, the book tumbled down, and she grasped the shelf with only one hand.

"Bless you!" Alexander said from somewhere else in the library, unaware of how close she had come to needing more than just blessings. She scrambled back into a secure hold, then carefully climbed down.

"Stupid book," she muttered, glaring at the book that had nearly broken a bone or two. She was very fond of her bones and had no desire to break any of them. Many children daydream about what it would be like to break a bone—to get to go to school on crutches, to have all their friends sign their casts, to get ice cream and attention and sympathy!—but Theo understood that the whole thing would be a giant, ice cream–flavored bummer.

And, worst of all, now she had no idea where to reshelve the book. It certainly didn't belong up on top of the shelf. Shame on whoever had shoved it up there. The spine revealed no author name, or even title. Frustrated, she shoved it in her bag. She'd figure out where it was supposed to go later.

Eventually she picked a book on the history of paleontology in America and curled up on a chair next to Alexander's couch, where he was confused but also intrigued, reading something by one of the many Brontës.

"Did you know oil is basically dinosaur corpse soup?" Theo asked, idly turning the pages. "So they can find oil deposits based on where dinosaurs would have lived and died and left behind fossils?"

Alexander looked up, wide-eyed, from his own book. "Did you know you should never dig up the corpse of your long-dead girlfriend and hang out with her?"

"I mean, I didn't think that was something that needed pointing out."

"Me neither."

"And I'll bet he couldn't even use her for oil, either."

"To be fair, we should stop using oil as an energy source anyway, so I suppose he has that going for him." Alexander grinned. He held his book out and pressed it against Theo's book on paleontology. "Look! We made a Brontësaurus!"

They snuggled in on each other's delighted laughter, feeling a little better overall. After a few cozy hours, Alexander's stomach reminded them what time it was, so they gathered up their bags and trekked out of the library. If it had been a normal library, an alarm would have gone off to tell Theo she still had a book in her bag. But it wasn't a normal library, and she had already forgotten about the book, much as she had forgotten about the special towel she'd borrowed from Edgar's shop. She never intended to steal things, but sometimes forgetful borrowing had the same result.

It had stopped raining, though the day was still sullen and cloudy. "Let's go have lunch with Edgar," Theo suggested. "I'm in the mood for a room-temperature, no-brand soda. And we can share our stuff with him, too."

"Good idea," Alexander agreed. Maybe Wil would be there. But even if she was there, she wouldn't really *be* there. It was weird living with an older sister whose focus was on them about 3 percent of the time. Normally they didn't notice it, because they had their parents to pay attention to them, but with their parents gone and Aunt Saffronia so Aunt Saffronia—y, it felt lonelier when Wil was there but never there. Alexander craved some sort of normalcy. At least he still had Theo.

"Maybe he has new information about Mr. Widow," Alexander said, though he was beginning to despair. It didn't seem like they had any clues. And he kept thinking about that letter from their mom. It *felt* like a mystery, but he didn't want to be in this one.

"Yeah. And maybe we can make Wil go on some

slides with us today," Theo said. Alexander appreciated how Theo said "us" even though she knew he wasn't going down any slides. It made him feel included.

They swung by the River Styx first to see if Edgar was there, but there was no lifeguard on duty. Normally that would make Alexander nervous, but as far as he had seen, there was no one in the park but them. If they weren't in the river, a lifeguard would be unnecessary, as there were no lifes needing guarding.

At the shop, Theo threw the door open and burst inside. "We bring real food from the outside, and—" She stopped cold. Alexander ran into her back, then stepped to the side.

Standing in the center of the room was a person who was definitely not Edgar. It was the man from earlier, the one who had been at the ticket counter. His mustache looked even meaner up close.

"What are you doing in here?" he asked, hastily replacing the bell jar he was searching under. By the state of the place, he'd been looking for something. "I mean, how can I help you?" He didn't sound like he wanted to help them, unless he wanted to help them walk down a dark, abandoned alley to some terrible end, or he wanted to help them rob a bank and then double-cross them and take all the money for himself, or he wanted to help them bake a pie that then turned out to have both meat *and* raisins in it.

"We're looking for Edgar," Theo said.

"I'm Edgar." He pointed to his name tag, which did, in fact, say Edgar. And was, in fact, Edgar's. Alexander knew, because where the smiley face sticker had been was now just the sticky circle left behind.

"No, you're not," Theo said.

"Yes," the man growled, pointing even more aggressively at his name tag. "I am. I've always been Edgar."

"You aren't Edgar! You're Edgaren't!"

"Okay," Alexander said, grabbing Theo's shoulder and tugging her toward the door. "Thanks! Bye!"

Once they were safely outside with a door between themselves and the person who was definitely not Edgar, Theo and Alexander turned to each other. "What's going on?" Theo asked. "Where is the real Edgar?"

"Whoever Edgaren't is, why didn't he just say Edgar was out for the day or somewhere else? Why insist that he's the same Edgar?"

"It makes no sense," Theo agreed. "Let's go ask him."

"No! No. I don't want to ask him anything. Maybe Wil knows where our Edgar is. Let's go talk to her." Alexander couldn't help but wonder: Employees weren't showing up for work. Mrs. Widow seemed determined to make the park awful. Edgar had argued with Mrs. Widow about new contracts yesterday. Add all this to Mr. Widow's disappearance. Was it possible everything was connected? But how? And *why*?

They hurried down the path to their cabasoleum, but Wil wasn't there.

"The library?" Theo suggested. Wil had been the one to direct them there after all. Maybe she had gone to look for them so they could have lunch together. But when they got there, the door was ajar and they heard loud voices inside.

"Where is it?" Mrs. Widow demanded. "This is the old Widow library. It has to be in here somewhere."

"Maybe those kids took it," Edgaren't answered in a harsh voice, like someone talking around a mouth full of gravel.

"Don't be ridiculous. What kind of kids would voluntarily go into a library?"

"True," Edgaren't agreed. "I'm only in here because you made me come, and I'm not even a kid."

"It has to be here. I need it. Keep looking." She sounded very angry. Theo and Alexander tiptoed away, not wanting to be caught and questioned about whether or not they were the type of kids who would voluntarily go into a library. All the kids they knew liked libraries; clearly, Mrs. Widow didn't understand kids. They should have expected nothing less from a woman who didn't have churros at a water park.

"What do you think she was looking for?" Alexander said, keeping his voice low even though they were alone in the cabasoleum as they pulled off their hoodies and jeans to reveal their swimsuits.

"No idea." And Theo wasn't lying. She had no idea that Mrs. Widow was looking for the very book Theo had forgotten she put into her own bag.

CHAPTER
ELEVEN

lexander wanted to spend the afternoon on the river, but with Edgar gone and Edgaren't taking his place, Alexander didn't really want to run into the large, mean man and his large, mean mustache. Just in case he decided to ask about whether Alexander and Theo were the type of kids who willingly went to libraries.

They headed to the slides, keeping an eye out for Wil. Alexander obviously wasn't going to go down any, but after overhearing Mrs. Widow arguing with Edgar about contracts, he was curious and wanted to sneakily question other employees. He'd start with the raft stand attendant.

But . . . no one was there. Not only were they the only guests in the park, it was looking like they would soon be the only people, period. Theo hopped the counter and grabbed a raft for herself while Alexander nervously looked over his shoulder, waiting to get in trouble.

"I wonder where the attendant is. Maybe it's because of the rain," Alexander said. "Or it's everyone's day off."

"Or maybe she was running . . ." Theo tried to make it sound like a joke, but the words hung heavy in the air between them. Theo cleared her throat and looked up. "Wait, is that Wil?" She pointed at the first slide.

"Are you trying to trick me into going up?" Alexander asked.

"No, it really is her. Come on." Theo hurried, and Alexander reluctantly followed. He didn't want to climb the tower, but he also didn't want to be alone at the bottom of the slides, just in case Mrs. Widow or Edgaren't came by.

And Theo had been right. Wil was at the first slide, leaning close in conversation with one of the seven identical lifeguards. Theo grinned at her and waved.

"Hey, Wil," Alexander said.

Wil looked over at them, a frown furrowing her brow. It was a look of concentration she usually only saved for her phone. "Have you two seen Edgar?"

"We've seen Edgaren't," Theo said.

"Not-Edgar," Alexander clarified. "Some scary man insisting he's always been here and that he's Edgar."

Wil turned to the pale girl. "Charlotte, is there anyone else we can talk to about it? Edgar was acting so strange yesterday afternoon."

"Everything has been strange," Charlotte said, squeezing the handle of her parasol with bloodless hands. "If they have their way, we'll have to go. I don't want to go."

"So don't," Theo said with a shrug. She set down her raft and entered Oblivion.

"What do you mean, if they have their way you'll have to go?" Alexander asked. Charlotte seemed very upset, and he didn't want to upset her more, but he needed to interview more employees if he was going to be a good detective. Even though he wasn't feeling good at detective work, or anything else, for that matter.

"We can only stay where we're wanted," Charlotte said. "We've been welcome here for so long. But now I'm afraid."

"Is this about the new contracts?" Alexander asked. "Is Mrs. Widow trying to fire you? Is that where the other employees went? Do you think she fired Edgar? But if she fired him, why is she pretending to have a new Edgar? Why does she seem like she's trying to ruin the park? What do you think happened to Mr. Widow? And do they really store things at the top of this tower?" All the questions burst out of Alexander like a gargoyle gushing out water to shoot someone down the slide. And Wil *listened*, which was the most unnerving part of all. She didn't even have her phone out. Things must be serious.

Wil put a hand on his shoulder. "Slow down, twerp. You shouldn't have to worry about this. You should just be having fun. Charlotte and I will figure it out. So go. Have fun. Take some candy from strangers." She smiled at him, but he didn't feel any better as he walked back down the tower stairs.

At the bottom, he found Theo staring straight up. "Look," she hissed. This time there was no mistaking it. There was definitely a figure—a person—behind the window at the very top of the tower.

"Maybe someone restocking?"

"Do you really believe they have storage up there?" Theo asked.

"No." There were more than enough buildings on the ground floor for storage. Even somewhere as weird as this place wouldn't think a ten-story flight of stairs was worth a little extra storage space. And Mrs. Widow had lied about there being a room at the top of the tower before changing her story. She didn't want them to know about it, so there had to be a reason.

Theo bit her lip, deep in thought. "Do you remember yesterday, when Mrs. Widow asked Edgar if he had seen Mr. Widow? It sounded like she thought that was a possibility."

Alexander's mind turned it over. "What if—what if he didn't get lost at sea? What if we were right the first time, and he's been in the tower all along?"

"But why?"

"He could be hiding. Like you said, his wife is a bully."

Theo nodded thoughtfully. If she was married to someone who combined raisins with meat, she'd probably hide, too. "Or maybe he went up there to get something without telling anyone or bringing a phone, and he got stuck. But that doesn't explain why he was seen running to the Cold, Unknowable Sea first."

"Either way, *someone* is up there where it doesn't make sense for someone to be." It was definitely suspicious. "Imagine if it *is* Mr. Widow, and we save him!" Everyone would be so happy to have Mr. Widow back. And it would make the wave pool far less terrifying, knowing that no one had actually disappeared in it. And it could improve this summer, solving such a big mystery. But Alexander didn't want to get his hopes up.

"Or it could be Edgar," Theo said. "Maybe they really do store things there, and he got locked in, and we'll set him free! Come on."

They hurried to the base of the tower. There was no door, which meant there were no stairs inside the actual tower. They climbed the twisting stairs around the outside, bypassing all the slides—none of which had lifeguards now, with no sign of Wil, Charlotte, or the other six identical lifeguards. But at the very top of the stairs, all they found was the highest slide. Alexander clung to the stone of the tower, staying as far away from the entrance to the slide as possible. He imagined the gargoyle face there turning and swallowing him whole, flushing him down a dark tube into the belly of the tower, which would be the same as the wave pool, only this time Edgar wouldn't show up to help him escape.

"Maybe we missed a door," Theo said, staring at the stone rock of the tower. She pushed on it, just in case, but it didn't budge. This was getting annoying. She liked being good at things, and she liked being fast, and this mystery was proving to be neither fast to solve nor something she was good at figuring out. She wanted to complain to her mom, but of course she couldn't do that, which made everything even *more* annoying. Annoying*er*. Annoying*est*. The bees and the ants were joining forces, creating a supercolony of agitation, and she *needed* them to be quiet.

They wound their way back down. Going down the stairs was much slower and much less fun than going down the slides and Theo resented every step. But even with their eyes glued on the tower, they didn't see so much as a window, much less a door.

"Mrs. Widow lied," Theo declared as they stepped off the bottom. "It can't be storage if there's no way to get in."

"But if there's no way to get in, how is there a person at the top?"

Theo put her fists on her hips. "One more look."

Huffing and puffing, they climbed all the way to the top. Theo examined the space around the top slide, but there was no ladder, no handholds, nothing. Even she wasn't bananas enough to try to scale the tower to reach the windows at the top. But she was a *little* tempted, all the same.

"Well, that's that. Nothing to see." Theo scowled.

"Not quite!" Alexander said, pointing over the railing. Down on the walkway, so far away they looked like a tiny toy of a person, was a figure running as though their life depended on it.

CHAPTER TWELVE

"That's how you disappear!" Alexander shouted at the person running on the walkway far beneath them, angry that there weren't any lifeguards here to say it. It shouldn't be up to him to keep other people safe, too!

"That's Edgar," Theo said. It was Edgar—the *real* Edgar. He was here, and he was running . . .

Straight for the Cold, Unknowable Sea.

"Come on!" Theo was chillingly certain they needed to get to Edgar before he got to the Sea. She pushed past the brass chain blocking the un-lifeguarded slide.

"Wait!" Alexander said. "There's no lifeguard! And we don't have rafts, and this is a raft-only slide. It has to be for a reason. Let's just hurry down the stairs."

Theo scowled, heart racing. They were going to lose Edgar! "Mom should have told *you* to be brave, not me. I'm not the one who needs it. You're still scared from the wave pool."

Alexander's face flushed a deep red of humiliation. And then he shocked Theo by pushing her out of the way and going first.

Theo threw herself down after him. Without the raft, she thought it would be faster. She was wrong. With their bare skin on the slide, they slowed, and slowed, and then . . . stopped. Theo bumped right into Alexander's back, both of them stalled on a curve halfway down the slide.

If the slide was mildly scary normally, at least it was over too fast to really understand how far above the ground they were. Being stuck halfway meant they had a clear, unobstructed view of just

how

high

they were sitting.

Water gently flowed around them, not enough to give them any momentum or carry them along. Alexander looked over his shoulder, his face perfectly calm in a way that surprised Theo. She had expected anger, or fear, or *something*.

"I told you," he said, his voice soft. "Mom was right. I should have been cautious." He then began scooting forward on his bum, inching down the slide, with a sullen and ashamed Theo behind him.

When the bottom was in sight, their skin itchy and red and painful from their agonizing descent, Theo whispered, "I'm sorry."

She didn't know if Alexander heard it, but his shoulders got a little less tense, and when he stood to walk the rest of the way down before jumping in the water, he held out his hand to help her up, too.

They swam across the landing pool and climbed out. They had lost so much time. "Where is he?" Alexander asked, looking around. In a weird way, the horrible slide had made Alexander feel a little better. Like he could trust himself again. Like being cautious was often the right choice and not just about being scared or nervous.

"He was heading toward the wave pool. Come on!" Theo started to run, but then remembered the warning about running, which felt far more dire now. She couldn't think of what to do, and she certainly wasn't going to advise against caution. Alexander had been right at the top of the slide. Her face burned almost as much as her poor legs.

But Alexander knew one of the benefits to always following the rules was knowing exactly what the rules *didn't* say. "Skip!" he shouted. It was almost as fast as running, and faster than walking. Together, the Sinister-Winterbottom twins skipped like their lives—or at least, Edgar's life—depended on it.

When they came around a bend and saw the Cold, Unknowable Sea ahead of them, they caught a flash of movement in the dark mouth of the cave.

"He's already inside!" Theo said, despairing. This was all her fault.

"Do we go in after him?" Alexander really, really didn't want to. But Edgar had always been nice to them. And when someone rescues you from both overwhelming waves and the horrors of meat-and-raisin pie, you owe them. Maybe you even owe them your life. Not because of the wave pool—Alexander would have been okay, eventually—but because who could say what would have happened if they had been forced to eat that monstrosity?

Theo's hand was already in Alexander's. They only held hands when they were nervous or scared. That meant she was scared, too, which made him feel braver. If Theo was scared, it was okay that he was scared. And it meant they could be scared together and still move forward. He gave her hand a quick squeeze to let her know it was okay. He was with her, even after the tower.

At that moment, as though triggered by their unity, the waves calmed and then stopped. Now it was just a pool with a creepy cave.

Theo flashed him a crooked, silly smile that made him feel less nervous. They crept along the edge of the wave pool, walking on the narrow ledge that circled it. Alexander was grateful at last that he had gone into the wave pool, because he knew exactly where to walk after having seen Edgar do it to help him.

They had to duck to get past the hanging stalactites, and then they were inside. It wasn't as dark as Alexander remembered it. The pool was luminescent, glowing a chilly blue-green. The only noise was the musical drip-drip-drip of moisture from the stalactites falling into the water, creating little ripples along the surface of the pool.

Alexander looked all around the cave. It was big, and black, and empty. Quiet, too, without the waves. There were no doors. The only way out was by scooting along the edges, and they would have seen Edgar leaving. "He's not in here," Alexander said. "And I can't see an exit. Where did he go?"

"Look," Theo gasped, pointing. Along the far edges of the pool, staining the glowing water, was a dark liquid.

"That can't be blood," Theo said, frozen.

CHAPTER
THIRTEEN

"That can't be blood," Theo repeated.

Alexander had the same thought. Not because it wasn't possible that the dark liquid in the water might be blood, but because that was too creepy and scary. Even holding Theo's hand couldn't combat that level of *bad*. He peered across the pool, trying to stay calm enough to think things through. "It doesn't look red. Or even dark red. It looks brownish-black. And would blood float on the water like that?"

"No," Theo answered, trying to sound more confident than she felt. But she had recently listened to a book about the human body, and it seemed like blood floating would be worth noting. She definitely would have remembered that detail. The dark liquid reminded her of something else she had been reading about, but she couldn't think exactly what. "I think blood would spread and dilute, not sit on top of the water."

Theo led the way as they inched around the inside of the cave until it curved back toward the substance in the water. It was also a good chance to check for hidden doors. There weren't any that they could see or feel, running their hands along the rough, rocky walls.

When they got to the substance, they hesitantly crouched down.

"Not red," Theo declared, relieved. And then she remembered what it reminded her of. "It looks like—like liquified dinosaur corpses!"

"Brontësaurus oil!" Alexander agreed, happier than he had ever imagined being upon seeing something making a mess. He watched as the oil slowly moved along the top of the water, slick and dark. He couldn't tell where it was coming from.

"Oil floats on water. That's how they find oil reserves sometimes. But why would there be oil in this pool?" Theo crouched down and felt the black rock right under their feet. It was damp, but her fingers came away clean.

Nothing had been spilled here and then dripped into the water.

"Maybe one of the engines that makes the waves is broken or leaking?"

"That would explain why Mr. Widow and Edgar both ran here. To fix a machine or to check on the oil spill?"

"But where did they go after they came in?" Theo turned around to continue their search. That's when she saw the dark figure in the entrance to the cave. And not a figure like the one they were looking for. A figure like the one who was insisting he had been Edgar all along, when, in fact, he was Not-Edgar.

"Where did he go?" Edgaren't growled, the sound bouncing off the walls of the cave and surrounding them, like he was wrapping his demand around their shoulders and shaking them.

"Who?" Theo asked casually.

"I saw him run in here! I was watching all day!"

"How?" Theo frowned. There was no way to watch the wave pool in secret. They had been on the tower, and he wasn't there. The only other view was from the cabanas, and Edgaren't definitely hadn't been in them.

"Who are you looking for? What's his name?" Alexander asked innocently, remembering how Edgaren't insisted he had always been Edgar.

Edgaren't clenched his jaw . . . and his fists. But he didn't say anything. He couldn't, not without admitting that he wasn't the real Edgar.

Theo gestured to the cave around them. "Only us." The waves started up again, slowly building, the noise making it impossible to talk anymore. Theo grabbed Alexander's hand and tugged him out the opposite side of the entrance from Edgaren't. As soon as they were safely outside, she whispered, "How was he watching the cave? *Why* was he watching it? And why is he looking for the real Edgar?"

Alexander shrugged, miserable. He couldn't help but worry Edgar was lost the same way Mr. Widow had been, and that it was their fault for not getting to him sooner. He should have insisted on caution, instead of feeling bad about being cautious.

Theo's face was downturned, her shoulders slumped in the same direction so it looked like her whole body was frowning. She should have trusted Alexander's caution, instead of insisting on doing it her way. Sometimes she got frustrated with how careful he was, but *he* always supported *her*. He had sat at the bottom of the slides and counted out loud for her after all. The least she could have done was listen when he said they shouldn't go down the slides without a lifeguard or rafts.

Now Edgar was lost, and Alexander wouldn't say it, but it was her fault.

"It's another mystery," Alexander said, trying to sound chipper. But while he loved reading about mysteries, he didn't particularly enjoy being part of one, he now realized.

Theo looked up at the clock on the walkway by the empty cabanas. Not a regular cheap plastic clock, but an actual elaborate grandfather clock, massive and looming. It chimed *doom, doom, doom, doom, doom.*

Closing time. Theo couldn't believe they had spent an entire day in a water park and done almost nothing but read and look for doors where there were no doors. "A mystery we'll have to solve tomorrow."

"If we can," Alexander whispered, still thinking about the dark mess of oil on water, the only thing they had found when they came looking for a friend.

CHAPTER
FOURTEEN

Wil was waiting at the cabasoleum for them.

"We think we saw Edgar," Theo said. "He went into the Cold, Unknowable Sea." Alexander pointed.

Wil stood up. "He's in there?"

"No." Theo shrugged. She didn't have any other explanation for it. But she was determined that, tomorrow, they would figure everything out.

Wil frowned, tapping furiously on her phone. "Okay. Let's go." They followed her through the empty pathways of the park. The rain puddles had evaporated, leaving only dry cobblestones. It felt *wrong* to be in a water park this dry, this lonely. Between the gloomy, rainy morning and the gloomy, mean Mrs. Widow, no one else had come at all. How was the water park supposed to stay in business like this? It was losing customers *and* employees—literally, in the case of some employees.

When they exited, the gate clanged emphatically shut behind them. Alexander looked back and saw Edgaren't there, watching them with narrowed eyes.

"How many more days do we have at the park?" Alexander swallowed against the lump in his throat.

"Three." Theo sounded less worried and more determined.

A ghost, pale and glowing in the late-afternoon light, stepped free of the trees. Alexander and Theo both jumped before they realized it was just Charlotte the lifeguard. She hadn't changed out of her weird bathing suit, and she still used her parasol as a shield against the setting sun, as though no ray could be allowed to touch her.

"They think they saw Edgar," Wil said, not looking up from her phone but somehow just sensing that Charlotte was there. "Going into the Sea. Didn't come out."

"But why would he—" Charlotte began.

Wil held up a hand to cut her off. "I'm on it. Listen,

twerps, Charlotte and I are going to hang out tonight. Slumber party."

"We are?" Charlotte asked, surprised. "But I don't sleep at—"

"We are," Wil informed her. "Tell Aunt Saffronia. I'll see you back at the park tomorrow morning."

Instead of walking toward the road, Wil cut back into the trees with Charlotte trailing her. Alexander watched them go, a worried feeling in his stomach.

"I think she's lying," Theo said.

"I think so, too," Alexander agreed. "But what is she lying about?"

"I don't know." Scowling and kicking a rock ahead of them, Theo led the way to the main road. Aunt Saffronia's enormous car was there, waiting. But Aunt Saffronia wasn't in it. Theo and Alexander looked at each other, confused, then back at the car.

Aunt Saffronia was in the driver's seat. They hadn't heard the door open or close. Maybe it had been a trick of the light. They got in and buckled their seat belts, trying not to slide around on the slick vinyl seats.

"How did you find the park?" she asked, drifting into the lane.

"Mysterious," Alexander answered.

"Aggravating," Theo added.

"Interesting," Aunt Saffronia murmured.

"You could come with us tomorrow?" Alexander asked. He thought maybe if they had a grown-up there, everything would make sense. Grown-ups seemed to have that effect on the world. Certainly things had made more sense when their parents were here. The world was much stranger—and surprisingly more sinister—without the elder Sinister-Winterbottoms.

"I can't," Aunt Saffronia said with a sigh.

Theo and Alexander blinked. They were in Aunt Saffronia's kitchen. They didn't remember driving down roads or getting to Aunt Saffronia's house. They must have been more tired than they thought. Even with the reading and sleuthing, they *had* done a lot of climbing.

"Why won't you come to the water park with us?" Theo asked, picking up on their last conversation.

Aunt Saffronia paused. "I didn't say I won't. I said I can't." She was poised on the edge of the room, and they expected her to drift out, but she paused. For once, it seemed like she was looking right at them. Her face somehow seemed both happy and sad at the same time, but she smiled. "Good night, dear ones. Sleep well and gird yourselves for what the morrow might bring."

Theo and Alexander ate silently in the kitchen, missing Wil even though she'd only be on her phone. Then they retired to their room. A jeweled lamp on the side table provided the only light, making their beds feel like lacy islands in the middle of a dark ocean. There was no television, no games, nothing to do except put on their pajamas and climb into their beds with the stiff white sheets and an unnerving selection of dolls arranged on shelves overhead, their faces tilted ever-so-slightly downward, as though they were watching.

"I wish she had books," Alexander said.

"Oh!" Theo remembered, at last, the one she had accidentally taken from the library. She reached into her bag and pulled it out. "Found this on top of one of the shelves. I didn't know where to reshelve it, so I put it in my bag."

"Wait. *Wait.* You stole a book?" Of all the things she could steal, it seemed extra bad to Alexander for Theo to steal a book.

Theo bristled at the accusation. "I *borrowed* it. On accident! Besides, it's a library. You take the books and then you bring them back."

Alexander took the book, feeling guilty for even holding it. There was no title or author on the spine or the dark leather cover, but when he opened it up, a handwritten title page declared it *An Account of the Widows of Fathom's End.*

"Fathom's End. Like Fathoms of Fun. And the Widows are the owners. This doesn't seem like a regular book; it seems like a family book. I wonder . . ." Alexander felt a twist of nerves. "Do you remember when we were outside the library, and Mrs. Widow was mad because they couldn't find something? What if it was this book?"

"I really didn't mean to take it," Theo said, feeling guilty, which then made her feel grouchy.

Alexander turned the page, expecting a table of contents and neatly organized chapters. Instead, he found a weird sheet of parchment with cursive so hard to decipher it might as well have been Elvish, and then page after page of what looked like contracts.

"This isn't a book," he said. "It's legal documents. Probably the deed to the park and stuff." Frustrated and understanding why Mrs. Widow was upset—legal documents were important—he handed it back to Theo. "We'll just slip it back onto the shelf tomorrow." Normally he would say they should admit what happened and apologize, but he didn't like Mrs. Widow and he definitely didn't like Edgaren't. Still, that didn't make taking Mrs. Widow's things okay.

Theo flipped through the pages, her eyes glazing over the contracts. Toward the back were weird, sort of mazelike drawings, and if Alexander weren't here, she'd probably pull out a pencil and try to do them. But he was watching her, so she put the book back safely in her bag. "No harm, no foul," Theo said.

"No harm," Alexander said, but he wasn't sure if he was talking about what had happened with stealing the book, or what he hoped would happen when they returned it tomorrow.

CHAPTER
FIFTEEN

I t was the strangest summer. It wasn't even that
their parents left them with no warning, or that
they were living with an aunt they had never
met before, or that they were spending their days
at a Gothic nightmare of a water park and trying to
solve the mysteries of the Cold, Unknowable Sea.

"Do you remember getting here?" Theo asked,
standing in front of the gate with Alexander. "Do you
remember getting in the car? Driving here? Could
you find your way back if you needed to? Could you
even say *where* Aunt Saffronia's house is?"

Alexander frowned. He had been thinking
about the same thing, but every time he tried to

settle his mind on it and work through it point by point, it kind of . . . drifted away, like fog disappearing in the morning sun, but *unlike* the fog all around them, which seemed immune to the morning sun. Every step toward Fathoms of Fun lowered the temperature of the air around them until they were nearly shivering.

"What were we talking about?" Theo asked, frowning at the ticket box. It had been something important, but now she couldn't remember it.

"I don't remember," Alexander said, shaking his head. "Look. Edgaren't isn't there. No one is there." A sign, in brutal, messy handwriting unlike the usual elegant script on signs here, said, *No new tickets. Park full.*

"Their limit is . . . three guests?" Alexander asked.

"Maybe a whole bunch of people came today and they sold out of tickets?" Theo peered through the gates. A gust of wind made the fog shift shiftily through the empty pathways between buildings.

"Yes, it's bustling," Alexander said.

"I wonder what Wil and Charlotte did last night?" Theo asked as they walked into the bustlingly empty park. She had never been to a sleepover. Their parents didn't allow them, but apparently Wil took their absence as a reason to ignore some of the stricter family rules.

Theo thought which family rules she'd ignore this summer as revenge since her parents abandoned them for the entire summer. She was going to eat ice cream before dinner. She was going to say the f-word, which in their family was f-a-r-t, a word their mother absolutely refused to let them say. She was going to ride a bike in open-toed shoes. Well, maybe not that. She really liked having intact toes. But she was definitely going to use electronics after 5:00 p.m., assuming she ever found electronics in Aunt Saffronia's house.

"Let's go check in with Wil and then make a plan for the day," Alexander said, who was oblivious to Theo's plans to rebel and had no such plans of his own. Just because their mother couldn't hear them didn't mean she wouldn't somehow just *know* they had said f-a-r-t aloud. "Besides investigating the Cold, Unknowable Sea, our plan should include how to return that book without being caught by Edgaren't or the Widow."

"And maybe Wil has heard from Edgar, or Charlotte has. Maybe we didn't see him run into the pool at all," Theo said. But her frown contradicted her words. She knew what she'd seen. Edgar ran into the pool, they followed, and he was gone. The itchy rashes on her legs from the slide fiasco were a painful reminder of her failure to catch him.

As they walked through the fog curling gently around their feet, they kept their eyes out for the crowds that would mean the park was full. There was no one.

When they got to their cabasoleum, Wil was nowhere to be seen. Her bag was, though, which meant she had beaten them. The towel Theo had borrowed and forgotten to return was there, too, crumpled on a chair. She smoothed it out, noticing an embroidered MW on the edge. "Mr. Widow," she whispered, wondering if that was why Edgar hadn't wanted to loan it to them. She felt a twist of guilt that she had taken it without asking.

"Should we go on the lazy river?" Alexander asked. He didn't know what else to do. He felt like they should be looking for Edgar, but they had followed their only clue to a dead end.

No. He didn't like the phrase "dead end" here. They had followed their only clue to an empty cave. That was all.

Theo shrugged. Normally she would be willing to disregard everything in favor of having fun, but there were too many things nagging at her. She didn't even know if she'd be able to enjoy a slide, worrying about Edgar and Mr. Widow and who was in the tower. And also, after yesterday's painfully bad slide experience, even she wanted a break from them.

"Let's go see what's on the menu for lunch today," she said. "Maybe it will be edible."

"And maybe Robert will be there, and know where Edgar is." Alexander hadn't been able to interview many employees, since they were basically all gone.

But when they got to the restaurant, it was closed. They peered inside. Everything was dark. Abandoned.

Because they were near the library, they tried the door so they could return the book before anyone noticed. But that door was locked, too. "We'll return it later," Theo said, frowning. She didn't like the way the park felt. They hadn't seen *anyone*. Not just no guests, but no employees, either. Much as Theo liked freedom, that didn't seem safe. Even her bees were wary and subdued, a low warning buzz in the background.

"Should we check the slides and the river for Wil?" Alexander suggested. He looked up at the tower, looming ominously, watching everything but holding its secrets tight.

"She spends most of her time at the cabasoleum. Let's just wait there." Theo didn't want to run into Edgaren't again. If he was still insisting he was Edgar, he'd be at the shop or at the River Styx, both places they'd need to go to look for Wil.

They retired to their cabasoleum. The Cold, Unknowable Sea's waves lapped hungrily just out of reach, a constant reminder of both the unknowable: what was happening or where Edgar was, and the very knowable: they didn't want to go back into that attraction.

Theo timed the waves, using the borrowed timer worn beneath her shirt. The waves were forty-five minutes on, five minutes off to give the nonexistent guests a chance to rest.

With nothing to do but wait, the morning crept along as slowly as a caterpillar inching across a busy road to either a quick smushing or metamorphosis into a butterfly—but more likely the former.

Bored with timing the waves, Theo paced the interior of their cabasoleum, counting her steps. Then she paced the exterior. When she came back in, she had a puzzled frown on her face.

"It doesn't match," she said.

"What doesn't?" Alexander asked. He was paging through the book Theo stole—or, as she put it, aggressively borrowed. It looked like mostly contracts, a page that required speaking lawyer but was probably a deed to the land, and there were also some weird drawings and sketches that looked like mazes. He was proud of Theo for not trying to complete the mazes. She *really* liked mazes.

"The dimensions of the cabasoleum." Theo was good at space. Moving through it, and understanding it, too. She liked geometry best of all the kinds of math, because it made the most sense to her. "The inside is smaller than the outside."

"Isn't that true of every building?" Alexander asked.

"But it's too much smaller. See here, the width of the stone at the entrance? It's half my hand, so fewer than three inches. The interior space should only be a few inches smaller than the exterior space. But it's not. It's three *feet* smaller."

"Where are we losing the thirty-six inches?" Alexander asked, now intrigued. He shoved the book into one of his jacket pockets. He always chose jackets with pockets large enough to accommodate books, because he was a smart and practical young man.

"Maybe the stone is thicker on the sides or in the back?"

"It has to be the back," Theo said. Because the front was open, she could put her hands on either side of the walls there, and they were a single layer of stone. Which meant the back wall was inexplicably ten times thicker.

"Why would it be that way? Insulation?" Alexander asked.

"Why would they insulate only one side of an open building?"

"Maybe there's wiring or pipes or something back there."

"There's no way to get in. I checked the outside. No panels or doors or anything. So if they did have wiring or pipes back there—which doesn't make sense because we don't have electricity or plumbing in here—they'd have to tear the wall open to get to it." Theo stared at the back of the cabasoleum. She remembered her sense the first day that they were being watched. She had shrugged it off at the time, but with everything that had happened since then, maybe it wasn't just a random paranoia. "Do you have a flashlight?" she asked.

"No. Wil would have one on her phone."

"Where *is* Wil?" Theo sighed. She sat next to Wil's

bag and started rummaging through it. She liked to steal Wil's gum whenever the bag was left unattended. Theo's fingers closed around something smooth and rectangular. It was a very normal object, but it filled her with terror. She slowly pulled it out, eyes wide, speechless.

"Is that?" Alexander asked, unable to finish the sentence. "It can't be."

"It is," Theo whispered, staring down at the impossible object.

CHAPTER
SIXTEEN

"Rodrigo." Theo was holding Wil's phone. Wil had left her phone in her bag. *Wil had left her phone.*

"Something is wrong," Alexander said, feeling sick.

"Very, very wrong," Theo agreed. Because there was no way—no way at all—that Wil would willingly leave Rodrigo behind. Which meant wherever Wil was, she hadn't gone willingly. She had gone won'tingly.

"Give it here," Alexander said, taking the phone. They didn't know Wil's passcode. But he could turn on the flashlight from the lock screen.

He swept the light along the back of the cabasoleum. The first pass didn't show anything. But on the second pass, he noticed something odd.

"Do you see that?" he asked. The circle of light projected onto the wall had a small circle of darkness in the center of it.

Theo grabbed a chair and dragged it over to stand on. "There's a hole!" she said, excited. She stuck her finger in. It went all the way through to darkness on the other side. There *was* a space behind the wall. She had been right.

Alexander handed her the phone and she shone the light through, but she couldn't see much back there. She could see enough, though, to know that the cabasoleum definitely didn't end where it should.

"What do we do?" Alexander asked. "Something happened to Wil."

There was no question in Theo's mind, either. Wil was in trouble, and Edgar was missing, and there was no one else in the park to help them.

"We could call Aunt Saffronia?" Theo said, but she sounded doubtful that it would do any good.

Normally, Alexander's innate caution would compel

him to turn to an adult. But for once, it didn't. "She said she wouldn't—*couldn't* come in the park. And even if she did, can you imagine her being helpful?" Alexander had a very good imagination, mostly used to visualize elaborate worst-case scenarios, but even he couldn't picture a way Aunt Saffronia would help. "We don't know how long Wil's been missing. It could be since last night or just since this morning. I don't want to waste any time waiting for Aunt Saffronia to get here." Alexander wrung his hands.

"The towel!" Theo cried.

"What do we need towels for? I don't want to get in the water!"

"No! Remember that weird rock design on the towel? It was the one Edgar set aside. And it has MW embroidered on it. Maybe it belonged to Mr. Widow." She grabbed the special towel and spread it flat on the rug that covered the cement floor of the cabasoleum. The bees were at a fever pitch of buzzing, but Theo didn't even mind. Sometimes she remembered how smart bees were. How they danced to tell each other where to find things. And right now, all her tangled, jumbled, buzzing feelings were lining up to tell her what to do and where to look.

"What does that look like to you?" she asked, pointing to the pattern on the towel.

"A rock wall, just like everything else here." Alexander frowned.

"Not just *a* rock wall. *Our* rock wall." Theo pointed it out, barely able to contain her excitement. The stones lined up exactly.

"Why would they do that on a towel? Is it like a map or something?"

"Or instructions. Come on." Theo grabbed one end of the towel and Alexander the other. They lined it up with the correct stones on the wall. "Look, the smooth stone on the farthest left of the towel has a faint star. See?"

"That lines up to . . . this stone." Alexander pushed, and to his surprise, the stone moved like a button. There was a grinding noise, followed by a squeal of gears that hadn't been oiled in far too long. Then part of the wall swung open, revealing a dark passageway.

"Well, *this* isn't on the park map," Theo said.

Alexander peered inside the space. There wasn't much back there. Just some hooks on the wall that held long poles with nets on the end, probably to clean out the wave pool. "Why do you think they have them hidden?"

"Ruins the look of the park, doesn't it? They don't

have anything like this where people can see it. I'll bet they have all sorts of cleaning and maintenance gear hidden around."

Alexander agreed. They were certainly dedicated enough to a theme to build secret compartments just to hide reality. He put his finger in the small spyhole. At first he thought what he felt was dust, but it was too gritty. It looked like bits of stone.

"It was drilled recently," he said. "Do you think someone was spying on us?" he asked.

"Only one way to find out." Theo grabbed the wall and swung it shut.

"No!" Alexander shouted, but it was too late. The wall clicked back into place, sealing them in.

CHAPTER
SEVENTEEN

Alexander ran his hands over the wall, but there was nothing to grab on to in order to pull it back open. "We don't know how to get out!"

Theo shrugged apologetically. Sometimes she acted too soon. But they needed the wall shut in order to see what the spyhole was for. She went up on her tiptoes and put her eye against it. "Interesting." It wasn't focused on the inside of their cabasoleum at all. It was focused on the entrance to the Cold, Unknowable Sea. As she moved aside to let Alexander look, she kicked something that went skittering across the floor. Taking the light, she searched until it reflected off a piece of glass. It also revealed a hole in the floor with a ladder leading downward.

Theo nudged her brother aside and put the glass against the hole. It was a perfect fit, and turned the spyhole into a spy*glass*, now trained on the inside of the Cold, Unknowable Sea.

"Why would they want to spy on their own wave pool?" he asked, confused.

"Maybe it's a secret lifeguard post?"

"They don't seem very concerned about safety. And even if they were, why keep it secret? Edgar stands out in the open to lifeguard the lazy river, and there were lifeguards posted at all the slides, at least on the first day."

"Edgaren't! We didn't see him watching the entrance to the wave pool, but he knew Edgar went in, and he knew we went in, too! He must have been watching from right here!"

Alexander shivered. It gave him the creeps, thinking of Edgaren't standing behind the wall, invisible to them. Maybe even listening to their conversations. Definitely spying on the Cold, Unknowable Sea. "I think you're right. But what should we do now?"

Theo was ready to get out of the confined room. There

wasn't any space to move, and she hated it. She pushed on the wall, then pushed again, then picked a different spot and pushed some more. No luck.

"The ladder?" She shined the light to show Alexander.

"The ladder," Alexander agreed, his voice filled with trepidation. He loved the word "trepidation," the way it took a long time to say, like you were worried about what each syllable would bring. It even *sounded* nervous. But he didn't love the feeling of trepidation.

Theo went down first, Alexander shining the light to guide her way. Then he dropped the phone to her, and she did the same for him.

The ladder, though old, was steady and securely bolted to the wall. Their fears that they would find a sewer or another small chamber with no escape were both soothed. Though the space down here could be considered sewer-like, it was more in the sense of subterranean tunnels than in the sense of oh-no-what-just-floated-past-my-leg, and there were absolutely no martial-arts-trained mutated reptiles to be seen.

There were distant sounds of dripping, but this portion of the tunnel was dry. It was made of the same stone as everything else around here, with sconces on the walls. Alexander searched for a switch but couldn't find one.

The phone flashlight only illuminated their way forward a few steps. "We don't know where this tunnel goes."

"Well, it has to go somewhere, right? Maybe Wil found the secret wall and ended up down here, too." Theo took Alexander's hand, and they began walking.

Alexander held the light steady, occasionally sweeping it from side to side to see if they were missing anything like light switches or doors or signs that said *This way to the surface, so sorry for the bother.* There were none to be found.

After what felt like an eternity, though, there was something else: branching tunnels.

"Which one do we choose?" Theo asked.

"I don't know. And I don't know how to know." Alexander wanted to sit on the cold stone floor of the tunnel. He wanted his parents. He wanted Wil to appear, annoyed they were holding her phone but happy to be found. As though summoned by thoughts of its owner, Rodrigo chimed.

Alexander glanced down at it. He couldn't unlock the phone, because he didn't know Wil's password, but he could see the text of the message on the lock screen. "What do you think 'Here are the blueprints you asked for' means?"

"It means someone is sending Wil blueprints." Theo shrugged.

"But why would Wil need blueprints? What are blueprints, even?"

"They're the way buildings are designed. And also . . . tunnels!" Theo clapped her hands together in triumph. "There are blueprints in the book we aggressively borrowed!"

"*You* aggressively borrowed it, not me. Do you mean those weird mazes at the end?"

"Yes!"

Alexander tugged the book free from his jacket pocket. One section had clearly been torn out—it made him shudder, thinking what kind of person you'd have to be to tear pages out of a library book—but before that were several pages of *blueprints*.

Including a detailed diagram of tunnels. But he couldn't make sense of them at all. He shoved the book under Theo's nose, training the light on the pages. "Can you read them?"

Theo frowned. But then she realized it was just the same as looking at everything from above, only smaller and flat. Like she was a bee herself!

"So if we started here," she said, finding where their

cabasoleum would be based on the long tunnel they had followed, "then we're here right now." She jabbed her finger at the intersection of three tunnels. "This one goes toward the restaurant, the library, the shop, and the ticket building. This one goes out of the park. And this one goes toward . . . the tower."

Theo looked up. Alexander met her eyes. Even in the dim glow of the flashlight, they could both see the *aha!* expression on the other's face.

"That's how you get into the tower," Alexander whispered.

"No," Theo said, bouncing on her feet in anticipation. "That's how *we* get into the tower."

Alexander wondered if they should go for the shop. Try to find Wil first. But if nothing else, the tower would be a way out, and he really wanted to know what—who— was up there. Besides, without knowing where Wil was, the tower was as good a direction as any.

They turned left, toward the tower. "What if," Theo said, talking fast and excited, "Mr. Widow is stuck? What if he found these tunnels, too, and made it to the tower but couldn't get back out? Or tried to but didn't have a map and could never make it out of the tunnels? We're going to rescue him!"

"Let's go save the Widow in the tower!" Alexander thought that if *The Widow in the Tower* was a book, he'd want to read it. And now he could imagine himself as the hero in that story.

But he was very, very wrong about what kind of story he was in.

CHAPTER
EIGHTEEN

"This is it!" Theo danced around the entrance to the tower. To think, the way in was *underneath* them the whole time! There wasn't even a locked door, or anything blocking them. Just an arched doorway, and beyond it, winding stairs going up and up into darkness.

"We'll have to come back *down* the stairs, too," Alexander said, suddenly missing the terrifying waterslides. At least they were fast, and you were falling on purpose. Unlike stairs, which were slow, and falling was very, very bad. Taking a deep breath, he began climbing. The stairs wound around in a tight circle. They had to go single file and carefully.

There was no railing and no light switches that Alexander had seen. This part of the park would never get safety approval, though he assumed it was never supposed to be seen by guests. He wondered who it *was* supposed to be seen by, though.

At the top at last, their legs burning with the effort, they found a small platform in front of a wooden door. The door looked like it weighed a ton, and was reinforced with iron bars. It was also bolted shut. From the *outside*.

Alexander frowned at the heavy bolt. Unlike the stone and wood, it looked brand-new. "If they store things here, wouldn't it make sense to have a normal lock that required a key? Anyone could slide this open and get inside."

"But no one inside could slide it open and get out." Theo bit her lip, suddenly nervous. "That has to be it, right? Why Mr. Widow couldn't get out? Maybe he accidentally locked himself in."

"From . . . the outside."

"Maybe someone didn't realize he was there and bolted it shut? And he hasn't been able to get out?"

"Maybe." Alexander wanted that to be the answer, but he suspected there was something else going on here. "Do we open it?"

Theo nodded, trying to look more certain than she felt. She liked feeling certain. Butterflies were pretty in gardens, but they didn't belong in her stomach. She was already full of insects; no room for more. She grabbed the bolt and slid it free, then pushed the door open. Their eyes, used to the gloom of the tunnels, couldn't quite adjust. There was a small room. There was the window where they had seen a figure. And there was a figure, backlit by the window.

The person turned with a gasp, then rushed toward them. Their eyes finally adjusted, and they saw not the expected Mr. Widow, but ... Mrs. Widow? Now she wore a long white dress, the hem of which was dirty and torn. Her eyes without the strange green glasses were blue and open very wide.

"Hello, Mrs. Widow," Theo said, deeply embarrassed. It *was* a storage room after all. They had been wrong and wasted so many climbs up so many stories of stairs. And now Mrs. Widow was going to get mad at them for snooping. "Doing, uh, inventory?"

Alexander couldn't even speak, he was so afraid, waiting for Mrs. Widow to shout at them for coming up the tower when she had told them not to.

"How do you know me?" Mrs. Widow cried out, then

looked at the open door past them. "Oh!" She rushed by, going down the stairs so fast she was a blur.

"Not Mr. Widow, then," Alexander said, relieved that at least they hadn't been shouted at. The now-empty room had a pile of blankets on the floor, and the remains of several meals on an overturned crate. Definitely not storage. It looked almost like Mrs. Widow had been living up there. Maybe that's why she had warned them away from the tower. She didn't want them to know she lived in it.

"Is it just me, or did she have no idea who we were?" Theo asked.

Alexander's happiness over not being yelled at had distracted him. But Theo had a point. "She could be bad with faces."

"It's not like there are so many guests in the park she can't be expected to remember individuals. And what was she doing up here, anyway? How did she get locked in?"

"Maybe it really is just storage and the person we saw in the window before was a different employee." Alexander was miserable with disappointment. He had already imagined emerging from the tunnels, a weary but grateful Mr. Widow at his side, the joyous reunion somehow fixing everything at the park.

But even then, it wouldn't have explained where Edgar went, or why Edgaren't had been using their cabasoleum to spy on the Cold, Unknowable Sea, or, most important, where Wil was. Alexander had hoped that by answering one question—who was in the tower—they would be given the answers to the rest of their questions.

Now, though, they had *more* questions. And ten flights of stairs to go down.

NINETEEN

Theo took the lead down the long, long stairs. Alexander was worried about the battery level on Wil's phone if they kept using the flashlight, but they were in luck: orange bulbs flickered to life along the walls.

"Mrs. Widow must have turned on the lights." Alexander was grateful for that at least. Maybe she wasn't as mean as they thought she was.

"Let's catch up to her and make her explain how she got locked in the tower. Maybe she knows where Wil is, too." Theo went as fast as was safe down the stairs, which was still faster than Alexander wanted to go. But by the time they got to the bottom, there was no sign of Mrs. Widow and her long white dress. At least the lights were on down here, too.

"Any idea where she went?" Alexander asked.

"She's probably leaving the tunnels." Theo checked their map. They already knew they couldn't get back out through their cabasoleum—or if they could, they didn't know how. "This way should lead us to Edgar's store. Let's try it."

Theo navigated until they came to a ladder leading up. "This should be it. Unless you want to keep looking around?" Theo held out the book to him.

"Climb up," Alexander said, not hesitating. He didn't want to stay down here. He hoped it was the right decision. Wil obviously wasn't in the tunnels, and Mrs. Widow didn't seem to be anymore, either, so he didn't see the point in staying any longer than they already had. He took the book and tucked it back into his pocket.

"Okay," Theo agreed. She was interested in exploring, but there were more important things to do. She climbed first, Alexander right behind her. But the ladder led into a dusty, tiny, pitch-dark space.

"Another dead end?" Alexander asked, trying not to listen to his brain telling him that they would never get out of the tunnels and would have to adjust to living there, slowly turning pale and hairless, like naked mole rats but with clothes on still. What would they eat? Where would they sleep? How would he ever see the next season of *The Magnificent English Confectionary Challenge?*

"Wait," Theo said. "There's a crack of light. I think this is a door! Push!"

The door swung open, and they tumbled out of one of the armoires. They were in Edgar's shop, and thankfully, it was empty. No sign of Edgaren't anywhere. Unfortunately, no sign of Edgar, either, or Wil for that matter. Had they really discovered secret tunnels and the hidden way into the tower only to find the one person they weren't looking for at all?

"Let's go to the tower," Alexander said, disheartened but determined. So they had followed the wrong trail. They'd find the right one.

"Again?" Even Theo, who normally had boundless energy, was feeling decidedly boundful rather than boundless.

"Aboveground this time! Maybe Charlotte knows where Wil is. Maybe Wil is there and this was all a weird misunderstanding."

When they got to the tower, though, they were disappointed. All the slides were closed, not a lifeguard in sight. Which meant no Charlotte in sight, which meant there was no Wil in sight, or any clues about where they might sight her.

"Maybe they're still together?" Alexander said. "Hanging out without us?"

"Maybe." Theo leaned against a railing and looked out over the empty park. From up here, it was all laid out like the blueprint map they had. Theo frowned. It was *almost* laid out like the map. But the map didn't cover the area around or underneath the Cold, Unknowable Sea at all. She retraced their tunnel steps in her mind but couldn't remember any turnoffs that would have taken them there. The tunnel from their cabasoleum went straight past it without a door or a turnoff.

Maybe there was nothing underground there. Or *maybe* those were the pages that had been torn out. But why?

"The park is going to close soon." Theo squinted at where the low sun was peeking out through heavy clouds. She didn't want to say it, but she had a sudden strong fear that if they didn't find Wil before tomorrow . . . they never would. She would be gone just as permanently and strangely as Mr. Widow and Edgar. This spooky park would have taken all three of them and given nothing back. But Theo didn't know what to do or how to solve this. Her bees had led her to *nothing*. Her mother told her to be brave, but what good was being brave doing her?

She didn't feel at all brave. She felt tired, and sad, and mad. Mad at this park, mad at her parents for leaving them for the summer, mad at herself for not knowing how to fix things.

"Theo?" Alexander said, swallowing heavily around the lump in his throat. He didn't want to say what he was about to say, but they needed to find what was lost. It wasn't a game anymore. It was *Wil*. "I think . . . I think we need to break some rules."

Normally, Theo would be thrilled to hear Alexander say this, but right now she just reached out for his hand. "Which ones?"

"All of them." He grabbed the phone next to the life-guard station at this slide, grateful that it worked, and dialed the number for Aunt Saffronia's weird wall phone.

"You memorized her phone number?" Theo asked, amazed.

"It seemed like a good idea. Besides, the numbers are like a date. Easy to remember." The phone rang several times before the ringing stopped and was replaced with static that made the other line feel very, very far away. "Hello?" Alexander said, not sure the call had gone through.

"You summoned me?" Aunt Saffronia sounded like she was in a wind tunnel.

"Hi, Aunt Saffronia. It's me. Alexander. Your nephew." He wasn't sure why he had to clarify that, but with Aunt Saffronia, it was probably a good idea. "Um. There's a special event at the water park tonight? It's, uh, a slumber party? Can we stay for it?" He braced himself for the flurry of follow-up questions he imagined were coming: Who was supervising? (No one.) Where would they be sleeping? (They wouldn't.) What would they do without toothbrushes? (Oh no, he wouldn't be able to brush his teeth!) Didn't he know that they weren't allowed to have slumber parties? (He did! He really did!) Did he know what the punishment for lying to aunts was? (He didn't, and he didn't want to find out.)

So he was shocked when Aunt Saffronia immediately said, "Yes, good. I'm . . . proud of you, Alexander. Remember, you need to find time. Good luck, children." And then the line went dead.

CHAPTER TWENTY

"Aunt Saffronia is a really bad guardian," Alexander said, frowning down at the phone.

"She bought it?" Theo asked, her voice shaped with disbelief. If her voice had been visible, it would have had huge, round eyes, and a mouth shaped like an O. As in, O NO THAT CAN'T BE TRUE. "How do our parents trust her enough to leave us with her for an entire summer?"

"I do *not* know." Alexander put the phone away and then checked Wil's phone, just in case there was a message there that would help. The battery was nearly dead. Wil would kill them. And he would be glad, because that would mean they were all back together. He took a deep breath, trying to focus. "Okay, so we can stay after closing. But how do we hide? We're the only ones here. Surely they'll notice if we don't leave."

"I have an idea." Theo led him to their cabasoleum. They grabbed their bags—leaving Wil's, just in case she was coming back for it—then walked out of the park. Sure enough, Edgaren't was looming near the gate. They could feel him watching them until they went around a bend in the path.

"Over here," Theo said, excited. She led Alexander through some trees to what looked like a sewer cover. "I saw this on the map."

"You can follow the map without even looking at it?"

Theo shrugged. "I just imagine I'm hovering above everything. It's easy." With Alexander's help, she tugged the cover free, revealing another metal ladder leading them back to the tunnels. "We take this to the shop, then hide in Edgar's snack armoire. We left the key there, re-member?"

"Right!" Alexander was impressed and also a little wor-ried about how good Theo was at this. First aggressively borrowing a library book, now breaking into a water park after hours. She was good at it, and he was going along with it. What was this summer doing to them?

Theo climbed down the ladder into darkness once more. Whatever the night ahead of them held, she would be ready. As much as she was worried about Wil and hopeful they would find answers, she was also excited to be investigating a mystery with her best friend at her side. She felt better now. Sometimes bravery came before the action, but she found it usually happened *after* she made the decision to do something scary.

The tunnels were much easier to navigate with the lights still on and the map in Theo's head. In the shop, the key was right where they had left it.

"Are we sure this is the best idea?" Alexander whispered as they pulled the armoire door shut. He was wedged in next to a bag of chips that crinkled alarmingly whenever he moved. "Maybe we should just find Mrs. Widow and talk to her."

"Did it seem like she was willing to talk to us? Besides, I don't trust her. She was arguing with Edgar the other day. She obviously lied about what the tower is used for. And she's up to something, trying to find that book of contracts and bringing in Edgaren't to replace Edgar."

"But she's allowed to be up to something! It's literally her park. She can do whatever she wants with it."

Theo grunted, part acceptance and part annoyance. She was sitting on several off-brand cola cans, and it was hardly comfortable and uncomfortably hard. "She's allowed to be up to something *until* it threatens our friends and sister. So I don't feel bad about doing any of this."

Alexander did feel bad, but he also agreed that this was their best option. He didn't think Mrs. Widow or that awful Edgaren't would actually help them. And he was convinced Wil and Edgar needed help.

They waited in the cramped armoire for an hour after closing, giving park employees—if there were any left—time to do their checks and cleaning, and giving the sun a chance to go all the way down.

"Should we take the tunnels?" Alexander asked.

Theo shook her head. "Mrs. Widow knows about them, and there's nowhere to hide if we're in the middle of one and someone's down there. If we stay aboveground, there are all sorts of alcoves and trees and shrubberies to hide in."

"Good point."

They crept out of the armoire, stiff and sore from their time inside. The shop was dim, most of the lights off. Fortunately, unlike the tower room, the deadbolt was on the inside. Alexander unlocked it and opened the door.

"Coast is clear," Theo said. They stepped out of the shop and onto the pathway.

That's when the lockets around their necks began screeching with alarms.

TWENTY-ONE

"What! Is! Happening!" Alexander shouted, trying to be heard over the terrible screeching of his locket.

Theo reached up and tugged hers free. "Take it off!"

"I can't!" Alexander fumbled with the clasp, but it was no use. He hadn't been able to take his off since they put it on. Neither had Wil. He was terrified. Obviously this alarm meant he was in trouble, and he desperately wanted to apologize to any adult who would listen for every rule he'd ever broken. (It was a very short list until today.)

They were going to be discovered. Alexander

took a deep breath. No. *They* weren't going to be discovered. Theo was holding out her hand, and Alexander wished he could take it. But instead, he grabbed Theo's alarm locket and shoved it into his jacket, then handed her the aggressively borrowed book and Wil's phone. "Go," he said.

"What? No! I won't leave you."

"Then they'll catch both of us! Hide in the tunnels. I'll tell them you're not here." It wasn't technically a lie, since he would be thinking about wherever he was when he said it, and Theo wouldn't, in fact, be right there.

Theo stomped her foot. "No! You need me. And besides, I—I already messed everything up. On the slide. If I had listened to you and been cautious, we would have taken the stairs and caught Edgar in time. None of this would be happening, I'm sure of it. We should be cautious!"

Alexander remembered the letter from his mom. As much as it made him mad, he also couldn't help but wonder if she had known something of what this summer held. "I'm the one who's supposed to be cautious. You're supposed to be brave. And this time being brave means running away. So be brave, and go!"

Theo hesitated, torn. She realized how much of her bravery was because Alexander was at her side. Because he looked up to her. Because he trusted her. She was brave because he was with her, and this time, he wouldn't be.

She would have to be brave alone. She threw her arms around him in a hug, then darted back into the shop.

Alexander ran in the opposite direction to put as much space between them as he could. He could barely see through his panic. Just when he thought he should slow down or he might get hurt, he ran right into the very broad chest of Edgaren't.

"Gotcha," the man sneered. Alexander had never thought sneering was a way to talk, only a facial expression, but somehow Edgaren't conveyed the same mean sentiment with his tone. Edgaren't pulled something out of his pocket that looked a little like a garage door opener. He pushed a button and the alarm around Alexander's neck—and the one in his pocket—turned off.

"Where's your sister, then?" Edgaren't asked.

"Which one?"

"The little one."

Edgaren't obviously knew he had two sisters, and didn't seem worried about where Wil was. Which meant maybe he knew exactly where Wil was. If Alexander had to get caught, he was going to get as much information as he could out of this brute.

"She's not here." Alexander figured it was okay to sound like he was terrified, because he was. Being scared right now made sense. "She was too, uh, chicken." Alexander was a terrible liar with very little practice, and this was the absolute least believable lie he had ever told. Fortunately, Edgaren't didn't know Theo.

Edgaren't snorted. "She might be a chicken, but you're a goose." He paused, waiting for some sort of reaction.

Alexander had no idea what he was supposed to say. He hated not knowing what adults expected of him, even though he didn't want to do anything that might make Edgaren't happy.

"Get it? You're a goose!" Edgaren't scowled, scratching his stubbly jaw. "Wait. No. I mean now your goose is cooked!"

Alexander thought Edgaren't needed to practice his insults a little longer before deploying them. Edgaren't grabbed Alexander's arm and led him roughly down the path, past the restaurant and the library, to a small building Alexander and Theo had never been in. Pulling a set of heavy iron keys from his belt, Edgaren't opened the door. Inside the building was a single small, dusty room.

And sitting on a bench, scowling, was Wil.

"Alexander!" Wil said, standing.

"Wil!" Alexander rushed into the room to hug her.

"No, wait—" she said, but it was too late. As soon as Alexander was out of the way, Edgarent slammed the door shut and locked it. Wil sat back on the bench with a sigh, then ruffled Alexander's hair. "What are you doing here?"

"We snuck back into the park to look for you. After we found your phone—"

Wil's eyes got a frenzied look, and her fingers spasmed instinctively around a rectangular shape that wasn't there. "Rodrigo?"

Alexander shook his head. "Theo has it. Anyway, after we found it in the cabasoleum, we knew something was wrong. How did you get in here?"

"I snuck back in last night to try and figure out what happened to Edgar and help Charlotte. But my necklace alarm went off and they caught me." She tugged glumly on her own heavy locket. "It's in the liability waiver contract we signed. That's why we can't take them off. Not until the end of our week passes. Where's Theo?"

Alexander pulled Theo's locket out of his jacket and handed it to Wil. "Hers always came off." He snapped his fingers. "Because she didn't sign her full name! She never does. Her contract wasn't legally binding." He should have looked more closely at the contracts in the book Theo aggressively borrowed. They might have given him some sort of clue. And he *knew* they should have taken time to read every single line of that stupid paper they signed to get their week passes.

He wondered where Theo was right now. If Wil's empty hand missed Rodrigo, his scared hand missed Theo. He hoped desperately she was being brave, wherever she was. "Did you find Edgar?"

"I didn't have time. I was waiting on blueprints. I have a theory about the Cold, Unknowable Sea."

"Someone sent blueprints to you!"

Wil sighed, leaning her head back against the wall. "Won't do me any good in here."

"We found our own blueprints. Did you know there's a network of tunnels under the park?"

"Interesting."

"And we got into the tower! We thought we'd find Mr. Widow up there, but it was just Mrs. Widow, locked in."

"When was that?"

"Not too long before the park closed."

Wil frowned. "That doesn't make any sense. She was in here with me all afternoon, asking questions about Edgar and whether or not he'd given me a book."

Before Alexander could tell Wil he was pretty sure they had the book Mrs. Widow was looking for, a small window in the door slid open, revealing Mrs. Widow herself. "Turn out your pockets," she commanded.

Alexander began to comply, but Wil stuck out an arm and stopped him. "Let us go. You can't keep us here!"

"According to the document you signed, I can, in fact, keep you here until the end of your seven-day pass." Mrs. Widow smiled, the expression mean and tight. She wasn't wearing her glasses, and there was something weird about her face. Other than her meandering eyebrows, which could have used blueprints of their own to guide them.

Mrs. Widow moved out of the way, and the door opened. Edgaren't stomped in, then patted Alexander down. He was glad he had passed Theo's locket to Wil, and that he hadn't kept the phone or the book.

"Nothing," Edgaren't said. Mrs. Widow, back in her bruise dress instead of the white one, scowled.

"Your eyes!" Alexander said, finally realizing what the difference was. "They were blue before." Now they were a murky sort of hazel.

"What?" Mrs. Widow said, her eyebrows wriggling upward.

"When we let you out of the tower, your eyes were blue. Did you put in contacts?"

"The tower," she whispered. "Heathcliff!"

Edgaren't turned and rumbled out of the room, followed by the Widow. She slammed and locked the door once more.

"I'm so confused," Wil said.

"His name is . . . Heathcliff?" Alexander liked Edgaren't better and resolved to continue using it. "What now?"

"I'll figure something out," Wil said, but she didn't sound hopeful. "I promise, twerp. I'm going to fix everything, somehow, just as soon as I—"

From beneath them came a hollow knocking noise, like someone trying to break out of a mausoleum.

CHAPTER
TWENTY-TWO

The knocking continued. Wil and Alexander got off the bench and peered at the floor. It was covered by a rug that looked like it belonged in a museum, if the museum was a museum of rugs so ugly they should only be displayed in museums for ugly rugs. They tugged the bench aside, then flipped the rug up. It actually looked better upside down.

"A hatch!" Wil cried out.

The door popped open, and Theo's very welcome face appeared. "Fancy meeting you here!" she chirped. She climbed up, her movement somewhat hampered by the very large tool she was holding.

"It turns out they really do have storage, but it's not in the tower. It's in the tunnels. I found bolt cutters." She beamed at Alexander.

"That was really brave of you."

"I had encouragement."

With Wil's help, they managed to snip the lockets off. Alexander felt much freer without it around his neck. "That's one way to break a contract," he said. Then he frowned, struck by a nagging thought. "We need to look at that book."

"We need to get you two out of here," Wil said. She ushered them both down and into the tunnel. Her cry of relief when Theo held out her phone was only slightly insulting, since it was definitely more emotional than she was when she saw Alexander again. But then her joy disappeared as she shrieked, "Those monsters!"

"What?" Alexander asked, panicked. "What did they do?"

"They turned off the Wi-Fi! And I don't have a good signal down here."

"We'll head for—" Theo stopped. She was going to lead them to the outside, but they heard heavy footsteps ahead of them, and then Theo's locket alarm—the one Wil still had in her pocket—began to go off.

They were standing at the intersection of three tunnels. The path ahead of them led out of the park, but someone was coming toward them from that direction. Wil looked down at the twins.

"Throw the locket and let's run!" Alexander said.

Wil shook her head. "No. I'm in charge of you two. I know you think I don't take it seriously, but I do. I love you twerps." She hugged them fiercely. "I'm going to lead him away. When he's gone, you take the tunnel out. Now hide!" She pointed to the third tunnel, then sprinted the opposite direction of the way out.

"What do we do?" Theo whispered. The footsteps were running and getting closer as the sound of the locket alarm moved away from them.

"Hide!" Alexander tugged her down the third tunnel. They ducked behind a brick support pillar, then listened as the footsteps continued, pursuing Wil.

"Edgaren't came from the tunnel out of the park, so he knows it's there. If we leave that way, we might not be able to get back in," Theo said.

"And we have no way of calling Aunt Saffronia, or anyone else. And I have no idea how long it will take us to walk to find help."

"And meanwhile, they might catch Wil."

"And no one will look for Edgar, or Mr. Widow." Alexander swallowed hard against the lump of fear in his throat. He wanted to run away, like Wil told them to. But he didn't think it was the right thing to do. There was a difference between being cautious and being scared. The scared part of him wanted to leave. But the cautious part of him understood that leaving would put other people at risk. People he cared about.

Even though staying was scary and technically breaking rules, it wasn't wrong. Rules were funny that way sometimes.

"So what do we do?" Theo looked at him for an answer. Theo usually plowed ahead confidently, not worrying about things like plans or rules. But this time, she very much wanted a plan. And she trusted Alexander to come up with a cautious plan that would help everyone.

Alexander snapped his fingers. "Contracts!"

"How are *contracts* going to help us?" Theo wondered if maybe all this stress had snapped not just Alexander's fingers but also his brain.

"The book! It was filled with contracts, right? Mrs. Widow is determined to get it, and we heard her fighting with Edgar about contracts. There must be something important in there, some reason why all this is happening." Alexander held out his hands and Theo passed him the book. They crept out of their dark alcove.

Theo paused, getting her bearings, then pointed. "That way to the library. We know they won't look for us there." She led them, climbing up a ladder and testing the floor hatch. It opened easily. The library was warmly lit with a few lamps, but no one was inside. They sat on the floor, heads bowed over the book as Alexander read contract after contract.

"So?" Theo said, bouncing nervously.

"Shh," Alexander said. "I'm reading the fine print." After several contracts, he looked up, eyes wide. "I figured it out."

"What?"

"The employees. They all have ownership in the park. Everyone from the lifeguards to the restaurant host to the chef. Not just the ones related to the Widows. Every single employee owns a percentage of the park."

"Doesn't seem like it would be worth much. No one is visiting."

"Yeah, that's true. But it also means Mrs. Widow can't sell the park without their approval. Maybe that's why Mrs. Widow wanted to renegotiate the contracts—so she can sell it and move on. If my husband disappeared in one of my water park attractions, I'd probably have negative feelings about it."

Theo nodded thoughtfully. "But it doesn't explain why she brought Edgaren't in, or why Edgaren't is insisting he's Edgar. Or where Edgar disappeared to. Or why they were basically holding us hostage when they caught us looking around. They're acting like guilty people, which makes me think they've done something wrong."

Alexander agreed. Part of being a rule follower was being able to recognize people who weren't. And Mrs. Widow and Edgaren't definitely weren't. He just didn't know *which* rules they were breaking, though now they had some idea of *why*. He turned to the back of the book, where the park plans were drawn and a few pages were ripped out. "I wish Edgar were here. I feel like he could explain everything to us."

"Wait, let me see that." Theo took the book. "Look, here—the section that's torn out. It's definitely the section that would be about the Cold, Unknowable Sea. So there's no way for us to see the layout or the structure. Or what might be underneath it." Theo looked up, eyes bright. "What if someone removed these pages on purpose, to keep it a secret?"

"A secret from who, though? Mrs. Widow? Wouldn't she already know?"

"If she already knew, why look for this book? And why make that spyhole to keep tabs on the cave?"

Almost every mystery they had started or ended with that cave. It was the last place they had seen their friend Edgar go, the last place anyone had seen Mr. Widow, and the last place Alexander wanted to explore further.

But Theo knew they had to have whatever secrets it held. "Only one way to find out. We need to go to the Cold, Unknowable Sea."

"I was afraid you were going to say that." Alexander sighed. But he tucked the book into his pocket and stood, resolute. "Let's try not to disappear, okay?"

They definitely would. Disappear, that is.

CHAPTER
TWENTY-THREE

The Cold, Unknowable Sea was even spookier after dark. It foamed where the waves crashed against the edges. Fog drifted and glowed with an eerie, sinister light. And not a Sinister-Winterbottom light. Just the regular kind of sinister, the kind that sends a chill up your spine, the kind that makes you think you'd really be better off turning right around and heading home.

But the Sinister-Winterbottoms couldn't go home, and they didn't trust Aunt Saffronia to fix any of this, and they certainly didn't expect help from any of the adults here.

No turning around. Wil had been brave. So would they.

"Wait!" Alexander said as they passed their cabasoleum. He pushed one of the lounge chairs against the wall, tipping it up to block the spy hole. Anyone spying would at least have to open the secret wall to get it out of the way, at which point Theo and Alexander would hear them.

"Good thinking! And while we're here . . ." Theo dug in Wil's backpack and found a plastic bag. She sealed the book inside. "Just in case we get wet, the contracts won't be ruined."

"I really don't want to get wet," Alexander said.

"Just in case."

"It feels like if you do something just in case, that case always ends up happening."

Theo rolled her eyes, but she smiled. "Well, better to be prepared than postpared, because you can't be ready *after* something happens, right?"

Alexander didn't want to waste any more time. He was worried the longer they delayed, the more he would realize this was a terrible idea. "Come on, the waves just went off." He charged straight ahead, skirting the edge of the pool. The hanging stalactite teeth of the cave mouth were black against the glowing blue-green of the water. Inside, it was so steamy it felt like they really *were* in a mouth. A mouth that was breathing, ready to swallow them.

"What are we searching for?" Alexander asked.

"Look, that stuff in the water. There's even more of it." Theo bent down, examining the oil pooling on the surface. "It's coming straight from the rock. It has to be. There aren't any machines on the sides."

"Wait." Alexander frowned, patting the book of contracts and blueprints thoughtfully. "Oil is worth a lot of money, right?"

"Yeah."

"What if . . . the oil really is coming from the rock? What if this whole water park is built on land that has oil under it?"

Theo caught on. "Then the land would be worth a lot more than some weird water park could make."

"And taking away a dozen employees' rights to that money would be worth enough to force them to change contracts."

Theo whispered. "Maybe even enough to make them disappear. They have one jail cell here. They might have more."

"We know Edgar ran in here. And Mr. Widow ran in here, too. And we checked all the walls. The only place we haven't checked is . . ." Alexander trailed off, staring at the water.

"The cave wasn't on any of the blueprints. Someone removed the details about it on purpose. Which means there's something hidden here." Theo peered into the water. "What if it's like our cabasoleum? What if the back isn't really the back?"

"I don't want to go in there," Alexander said.

"I don't, either," Theo admitted. None of this had gone how Theo imagined. Not just the lack of churros, or the park in general. It made her sad that she was looking at a wave pool and actually feeling scared-scared instead of excited-scared. Someone had *ruined* this water park. And as weird as Fathoms of Fun was, as melancholy and odd, it also had the best slides she had ever been on, and a new friend in Edgar, and what should have been an exciting, adventurous week with her brother and sister.

Whoever ruined it, whoever wanted to make other people suffer just to get more money? They were a person she didn't like. She wanted to fix this. She wanted to ruin their ruining plans. She wanted to get back at them for locking Wil in a room, for making Alexander scared, for *denying her churros*.

But she also wanted her brother to be safe and happy. "If you want," she said, "we can go. Get out of the park, call Aunt Saffronia, get Wil, and let whatever's going on here work out however it's going to without us."

Alexander was quiet for a long time. And then Theo felt his hand slip into hers.

"No," he said. "However it's going to work out is a bad way, and I don't want that. It's time to figure out what, exactly, is in the Cold, Unknowable Sea."

The steam had dissipated, and from outside, fog rolled in. It muffled the night, made them feel sealed off from the outside world. The fog drifted around their feet, clinging greedily, like it wanted to pull them into a watery grave.

And maybe, this being the worst summer ever, it would actually end that way.

"To save Wil," Theo whispered.

"To save our friends," Alexander whispered.

"To save—well, let's just do those two first and worry about the rest if we survive." Theo was always practical that way. Her brother nodded. They clutched each other's hands and took a deep breath. Then they jumped into the pool, glowing green and hungry beneath them. Their dark hair floated behind them as they sank, slowly, to the bottom, took a few steps ...

And then disappeared.

CHAPTER
TWENTY-FOUR

Alexander surfaced first, gasping less out of a need for air and more out of surprise. Theo followed, her face glowing with delight.

"It was an optical illusion!" she said. The back wall of the *cave* they had explored earlier was solid. The back wall of the *pool*, however, wasn't. It looked solid from above water, but once they were underneath, they saw that there was a narrow passageway. If the waves were on, it would have been impossible to find. But with the waves off, Theo had noticed the lines right away. It was only a few quick swimming strokes to go under the cave wall, and they surfaced in another room entirely.

There was machinery back here, which Alexander had expected. They had to generate the waves somehow. But there was also a staircase leading down somewhere else. Alexander and Theo climbed out of the pool and walked toward it. It wasn't like the ladders or the tunnels, where everything was old and rusting. The handrail was polished wood, the stairs beautiful black and white tile. They were lit by glass wall sconces.

"Careful you don't slip," Alexander cautioned. They were, after all, soaking wet.

"Here." Theo pointed to a shelf, where big fluffy towels were waiting. They wrapped up, shared a bemused look, and went down the stairs. At the bottom, they weren't greeted with another tunnel. They were greeted with . . . a living room.

"Living room" didn't feel like a fancy enough term. Alexander had read about parlors, and this seemed like a parlor. The sofas were dark green velvet, placed around a beautiful Turkish rug with a claw-foot coffee table so polished it perfectly reflected the chandelier overhead. The room was empty, but there were a few doors leading away.

"Which one do we go through?" Alexander asked.

Before they could choose, a door opened, revealing a bright kitchen behind a short, round man. He wore a pin-striped suit with a lavender scarf and had tiny, round glasses that magnified kind, round eyes.

"Oh. Oh!" He dropped the silver platter. A teapot and several delicate cups delicately broke into several pieces.

"Mr. Widow, are you all right?" a familiar voice asked. Edgar appeared behind him. "Theo! Alexander!" He looked at the stairs as though expecting the third Sinister-Winterbottom sibling to appear, but his face fell when he realized Wil was not there.

"Edgar?" Theo asked.

"Mr. Widow?" Alexander couldn't believe it. They had found both the missing man and the missing friend. "What are you doing down here?"

"Waiting, of course," Mr. Widow said. "Just like I'm supposed to. I'll go and get more tea." He scooped up the tray and the broken pieces, then disappeared back into the kitchen.

Edgar sat on the edge of one of the sofas, his face miserable. "*I'm* not waiting. I've been trying to convince him to come out, but he won't do it."

Theo flopped onto a fancy armchair, not caring that

her wet clothes would soak through it. "You mean he's just been hanging out in here, the whole time, while everyone thought he was missing? While Mrs. Widow had him declared dead?"

Edgar nodded. "I thought I was going to save the day when I found those blueprints in the library book and discovered a secret chamber beneath the wave pool."

"You're the one who tore the pages out!"

"Yes." Edgar blushed. "Please forgive me for harming a book. But I didn't want anyone to follow me until I knew what I was going to find. And I found exactly what I hoped for, but I can't get him out. And I'm afraid to go out myself without him, now that Heathcliff is here."

"Who?" Theo asked.

"Edgaren't," Alexander responded. Theo hadn't heard Edgaren't's real name, because she had been bravely fetching the bolt cutters.

"Edgaren't?" Edgar asked.

"Because he's not Edgar." Theo ignored Edgar's continuing confusion. "Why won't Mr. Widow leave? Is he afraid of Edgaren't, too?"

"No." Edgar shook his head. "He's obeying his wife's wishes."

Alexander felt like he *should* have a headache, even

though he didn't. "Mrs. Widow told him to come down here? But when we heard her talking to you, it sounded like she really didn't know where he was. And if she knows he's down here, why have him declared dead?"

"I know! I don't understand any of it." Edgar leaned back with a sigh.

Mr. Widow appeared with a new tea tray, this time with four cups. He set them on the coffee table, then poured tea for each of them.

"I don't suppose you have soda?" Theo asked. Then, since they had found two of the things they had desperately been searching for, she tried her luck at the thing she wanted most (after Wil's safety, of course). "Or churros?"

"What is a churro?" Mr. Widow asked, passing her a cup of tea and a hard cookie that looked like it had been freshly baked in the 1830s.

Theo slumped. She didn't even pretend to be interested in the tea, just set it back on the table. Alexander made more of an effort, but he had never really understood the appeal of tea. It seemed like something he ought to like, but he hadn't learned how to yet. Like brussels sprouts or shows about people looking for houses to buy. Someday he would grow out of all his clothes and into liking things like tea and miniature cabbage veggies and people insisting they knew what mid-century modern architecture looked like and couldn't live in anything else. But today was not that day.

"Mr. Widow, why are you here?" Alexander asked. "Everyone thought you were missing. Dead, even."

"I'm doing exactly what I'm supposed to."

Edgar rubbed his forehead. It was clear that, unlike Alexander, who felt like he ought to have a headache but didn't, Edgar felt like he ought to have a headache and definitely did. "According to Mr. Widow, many years ago his wife instructed him to retreat here if things ever got, and I quote, 'Weird.'"

"Um," Theo said. "Have you seen your water park? I think weird is the default around here."

"You misunderstand." Mr. Widow cleared his throat. He had a gentle voice, soft brown eyes, and the manners of someone who had never harmed a fly. He had not, in fact, ever harmed one, which was very aggravating to everyone who shared a kitchen with him. "Many years ago, when we first designed and opened our dream together, this wonderful park, my dear wife told me that if things ever seemed wrong, if she began acting odd or doing inexplicable things, I should retreat here and wait for her to come and get me. She has never led me astray. I will not doubt her now. I promised I would wait for her, and wait I will."

Theo leaned forward, intrigued. "So what made you come here?"

Mr. Widow's brow furrowed in pain and worry. "It happened so suddenly. She began wearing those odd green glasses, hiding her beautiful eyes. And then she hated Fathoms of Fun. It was her dream! Our dream together! She could never hate it, and yet she was pressuring me to figure out how we could sell it. And, strangest of all, she—" He paused, shuddering, looking as though he was going to be ill. "She . . . she suddenly liked raisins." He looked up at them, tears in his eyes. "Why would she do that? Why would she like raisins? It was as though I was looking at my wife but seeing a stranger. So I retreated here. I've been waiting ever since. She knows exactly where I am. Why hasn't she come for me?"

"Hold on," Alexander said, his mind whirling. "You said it was like looking at your wife but seeing a stranger." The Widow in the tower, without the glasses, had blue eyes. And the Widow at the cell, without the glasses, had hazel eyes. "What if," he said, heart racing as the pieces fell into place, "she really *was* a stranger? What if Mrs. Widow isn't Mrs. Widow at all?"

CHAPTER
TWENTY-FIVE

"What do you mean?" Theo asked. "How could Mrs. Widow not be Mrs. Widow?"

"Does she have a sister? Maybe a twin?" Alexander asked.

Mr. Widow frowned. "She never spoke of her life before we met. She said some things were best left buried in the grave of the past. All I know is that she was happy by my side and that we built our dream water park together. Why hasn't she come for me? I don't understand." His face fell, and he looked so impossibly sad that Theo and Alexander both felt it with him. The person he loved and trusted most in the world hadn't come for him, but he loved and trusted her enough to just wait.

Still. Theo could never stand to wait for anything. "There's only one way to prove Alexander's theory. We have to figure out whether or not there are in fact two Mrs. Widows." She paced. "We have Alexander, me, Edgar, and Mr. Widow. Wil is probably back in that same cell by the library if Edgaren't caught her. I have a map of the park in my head and Edgar's timer. What are our other supplies?"

Alexander checked his pockets. "I have the book with the real contracts, deed, and blueprints."

"I have keys," Edgar said, jingling his enormous key ring. "I can get Wil, and anything out of the shop, or any of the other buildings."

"But just getting Wil won't help us. We need a way to lure Mrs. Widow and Edgaren't out of the park, and make sure they can't lock any of us up. We have to be brave *and* cautious," Alexander said. He clapped his hands, a sudden idea striking him. "What if . . . there were *more* than two Mrs. Widows?"

"What? First there was one, now two, now even more?" Mr. Widow asked. "Is this young man . . . well?" He gave Theo and Edgar a worried look.

Alexander grinned. "If there are two Mrs. Widows and they had one locked in the tower, that would explain why they were so panicked when we said we let her out. They dropped everything to find her. So we're going to do that to them again."

Theo, catching on to his idea, laughed. It was a perfect plan.

"Okay. First things first: we need a few doors opened." Alexander turned to Edgar and outlined what they would do. It was risky, but it was their best chance at solving whatever was happening in Fathoms of Fun and hopefully, maybe, returning it to its weird fun self instead of the creepy cage it had become.

The first Widow in a long white dress appeared, wandering at the base of the tower.

The second, emerging from cabana 13.

The third, standing on the steps of the library.

The fourth, creeping from the shadows around Edgar's shop.

The fifth, lurking near the Cold, Unknowable Sea.

One of them checked a timer, then let out a piercing

cry like a seagull. They began running at once, flashes of white movement in the dark night.

"Hey!" Edgaren't shouted near the tower. "She's out again!"

"I see her!" Mrs. Widow shouted, near the library.

"I'm after her!"

"No, I'm after her!"

Because it was dark and the Widows in white were running very fast, it was difficult to notice that two of them were rather short. Four of them held parasols over their heads so they couldn't quite be seen. One of them ran with a cell phone clutched in her hand as though her life depended on it. One of them was rounder than Mrs. Widow, and that one slipped into the darkness of cabana 13 rather than running for the entrance to the park.

And one of them was laughing her head off, exhilarated to finally be allowed to run inside a water park. Edgaren't huffed and growled as he chased that one. The gleeful Widow in white ran even faster, pumping her legs, feeling like the wind itself. She had never run in a full-length dress before, and while it took some getting used to, she actually liked the way it trailed behind her, whipping around her legs.

Well, she liked it until it tangled in her tennis shoes and made her trip. She went flying, her fall kindly broken by a rosebush that promptly snagged every square inch of her lace dress.

"I got her!" Edgaren't shouted, grabbing the Widow in white roughly by the shoulders and pulling her free of the thorns.

"Do you, though?" Theo said, still laughing.

Just then, a Widow in white streaked past, running for the exit. Growling in rage, Edgaren't let go of Theo and ran after the new Widow in white.

"Get out!" Theo shouted. "Past the gate!"

Then she took another path, just in case Mrs. Widow wasn't chasing a Widow in white yet.

But she needn't have bothered. Mrs. Widow was quite busy. Ahead of her, a Widow in white darted onto the path, and Mrs. Widow charged at her. Then that Widow in white disappeared into the shop and before Mrs. Widow could barrel in, the Widow in white was somehow ahead of her on the path again, racing for the exit.

"Heathcliff!" Mrs. Widow shouted. "She's going for the exit!"

"I know!" he shouted from another part of the park. "I'm chasing her!"

"No, you idiot! I'm chasing her!" With a shriek of rage, Mrs. Widow ran as fast as she could in her own bruise-colored dress, which, fortunately for the Widow in white ahead of her, was not actually fast at all.

Her Widow in white led her around a bend, at which point another Widow in white sprinted out of the park, followed by Edgaren't. But Mrs. Widow didn't see that. And then her Widow in white went back to the main path and straight out of the park.

Mrs. Widow burst free of the park. Then she stopped, confused. Ahead of her she saw Edgaren't, holding not one but two Widows in white's arms. (They were not Widows at all, but rather preteens in white.) Before she could puzzle it out, the water park gate slammed closed behind them, and Edgar, wearing a long white dress, locked it tight.

"Hello," Wil said, climbing out of the tunnel exit and shrugging off the white dress she wore. "You have several crimes to answer for, including kidnapping, child endangerment, false imprisonment, and turning off the Wi-Fi."

"And no churros!" Theo added.

Mrs. Widow laughed, the sound small and mean. "You think this changes anything? All it does is solve the problem of where Edgar is and get you little rats off my land. Edgar will sign his new contract if he knows what's good for him, and tomorrow Mr. Widow will be officially declared dead. Everything will be mine. Heathcliff, open the gate."

Edgar stood in front of it. Wil stood next to him, linking arms.

Edgaren't-slash-Heathcliff held one of Alexander's arms and one of Theo's. "But what do I do with these kids?"

"It doesn't matter!"

"No," Edgaren't said, sounding very certain and suddenly far scarier. "These kids matter a great deal, whether you know it or not."

Mrs. Widow ignored him. "It was all a trick! The four of them didn't accomplish anything, as long as—"

"Five," Alexander said.

"What?" Mrs. Widow snapped.

"There were five of us. You didn't catch one, because he wasn't running for the gate."

Mrs. Widow turned toward the park, a look of horror on her face as not one, but two white-clad figures slowly approached, hand in hand, drifting toward them on the fog as though coming from the grave.

Or, in this case, the tower.

CHAPTER
TWENTY-SIX

There was one Mrs. Widow on the outside of the gate, and another Mrs. Widow on the inside, standing next to the fake Mrs. Widow who was Mr. Widow, thus revealed as he took off his flowing white dress.

"She has an evil identical twin!" Wil said, shaking her head in wonder. It was astonishing enough that she wasn't even looking at her phone.

"Evil fraternal twin," the Mrs. Widow on this side of the gate snapped. "Though the resemblance is enough that I almost pulled it off."

"Agnes," the real Mrs. Widow said, shaking her head sadly. "You would never have pulled it off."

"I would have!" the fake Mrs. Widow shrieked. "And you're a fool, Jane, keeping this ridiculous water park open when you could sell the land for the oil!"

"When Father died, you impersonated me and took the jewels and the houses and the money. You left me with nothing. But I found love, and together, we took this place that no one wanted and turned it into something truly sublime." She still held Mr. Widow's hand. He looked beside himself with relief. He had been right to trust his wife all along, even if the last person he had thought was his wife was someone else entirely.

"It doesn't matter!" Fake Mrs. Widow said, reaching into her dress and pulling out a bundle of papers. "I got everyone to sign away their rights already!"

"Not everyone," Edgar said. "I never signed, so it doesn't matter if you had that man impersonating me. And if everyone else signed, all that means is I now have rights to half the land. And I'll never give it up."

"I'm so proud of you," the real Mrs. Widow said, smiling.

Alexander frowned. "Wait. If Mrs. Widow is your aunt, then that means fake Mrs. Widow is . . . your aunt, too?"

Edgar shook his head. "No, I'm related to Mr. Widow's side of the family. I didn't know my aunt had a sister."

"We hadn't spoken in years until Agnes showed up." Mrs. Widow put an arm around her husband's shoulder. "I always feared she might come, which was why I gave my husband such a cryptic warning. It's not the first time she's pretended to be me. And after what happened with Frank, and my poor, sweet—" Mrs. Widow shuddered, cutting herself off. "I wasn't going to risk it again, but I didn't want to trouble my dear husband with fears that might never come to pass. Still, I should have known better. Agnes was never satisfied with what she had, always wanting more. How she knew there was oil under the park, I can't understand. The only person who knew was the man I hired to clean up the leak, and—"

Edgaren't was slowly backing away.

"Wait a minute! It was you!" Mrs. Widow pointed at him. "How did you know to contact my sister?"

Edgaren't smiled, but it wasn't a happy smile. It was a jack-o'-lantern smile, brutally carved with something wicked burning behind it. "That's my cue." He turned and ran into the woods.

Fake Mrs. Widow threw the worthless new contracts

on the ground, stomping on them. "It should be mine! It should all be mine!"

"If you had asked, I would have given you a job," Mrs. Widow said.

"In this absurd park? Don't be ridiculous! I don't want a job. I want money!"

"Now you'll have neither," Theo said, folding her arms.

"Come inside and let's talk," the real Mrs. Widow said, her expression sad. It was easy to tell them apart now. The real Mrs. Widow's eyebrows, while still drawn on, were soft and kind, like her expressions. And when she talked, it didn't look like she was sneering or secretly plotting your demise. It looked like she cared.

"Never!" The fake Mrs. Widow turned and ran after Edgaren't, stumbling and tripping on the hem of her bruise-colored dress, doubtless incurring actual bruises beneath it.

"Do you want to go after her?" Edgar asked.

Mrs. Widow shook her head. "She's my sister, even after everything. And now everyone knows who she is, so she can't hurt us like this again." She opened the gate, coming out and embracing Edgar. "Call everyone back. We need them so we can get this park up and running in its true, glorious form once more." She turned to the

Sinister-Winterbottom siblings. "And you three! If it hadn't been for you, I don't know what might have happened. How can I ever repay you?"

Wil just shrugged, eyes back on Rodrigo. "Tell Charlotte she can stay, then turn the Wi-Fi on again and I'm good."

"You've seen Charlotte?" Mr. Widow looked shocked, then thoughtful as he nodded. "She and her sisters are always welcome here. Any other requests?"

"We still have a couple days left on our week passes," Theo said. "So as long as the park is open tomorrow, that's enough. We have a lot of fun to make up for. *Fathoms* of fun to make up for."

"No," Alexander said, his voice emphatic. Theo turned to him, surprised. It wasn't like Alexander to ask for things, and she thought solving the mystery was enough of a reward. Alexander smiled, though. "There *is* one more thing you can do for us."

CHAPTER
TWENTY-SEVEN

Alexander sat on the edge of the Cold, Unknowable Sea, feet in the water, face tipped back to the sun that had finally decided to grace them with its presence.

"You really are a good brother," Theo said, but it was hard to understand her. Her face and hands were coated with cinnamon and sugar, and her mouth was full of delicious fried dough in its most perfect form: the churro.

It still wasn't a normal water park, but it was a better water park now that it wasn't being run by an evil twin. In addition to a sun-soaked two days spent going down the slides (with rafts, this time, and even Alexander did a few slides), floating on the river, and finally taking advantage of the wave pool, their time had been filled hanging out with new friends. Edgar was back, and the park was bustling with families and kids their own age for Theo to race. There were also new lifeguards, who had apparently all been fired by the fake Mrs. Widow right before the Sinister-Winterbottoms arrived. Theo and Alexander kept an eye out for Charlotte or any of her six identical sisters but didn't see them.

Best of all, though, there were no more raisin-meat pies. *And* the chef had agreed that churros needed to be added to the menu forever, in their honor.

"I'm still mad at Agnes for giving fraternal twins a bad name," Alexander said as he carefully cleaned his fingers to get rid of the lingering churro crumbs.

"Well, I'm sure she'll regret it when she finds out the park has churros now and she can't come back in."

"I wonder where Edgaren't ran off to and if they're together somewhere."

Theo twisted her mouth, a surge of anger at the reminder. "And we still don't know how he found Mrs. Widow's sister, since not even Mr. Widow knew she had one." It bothered her. All the other mysteries were solved, but that one was out of her reach.

"Come on!" Wil shouted from their cabasoleum, packing their things. "Aunt Saffronia will be here any minute."

Edgar was waiting for them outside the shop. "Thank you," he said as he walked them out of the park, shyly adjusting his tie as he darted a glance at Wil. "Without the three of you, who knows what would have happened. Meeting you three has improved a very lonely summer, what with my dads gone."

"*Gone* gone, or . . . ?" Theo asked.

"I've worked here before, but this time they dropped me off at the park in the middle of the night, told Charlotte to take care of me, and left. I haven't heard from them since." He frowned, troubled.

"We know the feeling." Wil reached out her free hand and squeezed his arm. "Don't be a stranger. You have my number. We're here all summer."

"Where is *here*?" Edgar asked.

"At our aunt's house. She lives in . . ." Wil trailed off, frowning. She looked at Alexander and Theo. They looked at each other. They couldn't quite think of it, either, or remember where her house was or how they got there.

A horn honked, startling all of them. Though there had been no car on the road seconds ago, now Aunt

Saffronia's enormous aqua beast was waiting for them. Theo held out the timer to return it to Edgar.

"Keep it," he said with a warm smile. "As a thank-you."

Beaming with relief—she really hadn't wanted to give it back, but even she would never aggressively borrow something from Edgar without returning it—Theo pulled it over her head to wear like a locket. But not a locket that would sound an alarm and let bad guys catch them. *That* type of locket was one they would studiously avoid from now on.

Alexander looked at the car. Charlotte was there, leaning down to speak with Aunt Saffronia. She glanced back at them and offered Alexander a smile before lifting a hand to wave goodbye. When she did, her parasol moved, and a single shaft of sunlight cut across her skin.

For that second, Charlotte . . . disappeared.

Alexander rubbed his eyes in disbelief. But when he looked again, Charlotte was gone. Aunt Saffronia honked once. She stared past them, maybe looking at the tower where Mrs. Widow had been trapped, or maybe looking at something else entirely. Who could say? "You're finished," she said, nodding distractedly as they got in the car. "You found it."

"I wouldn't call Mr. and Mrs. Widow an 'it.'"

"Who are they? I meant *that*." She gestured vaguely in Theo's direction.

Theo's hand went around the timer. "This? I've had it for days. I never lost it."

"You've had it for days?" Aunt Saffronia sounded aghast. "Then why did we keep returning?"

"To . . . solve the mystery?" Alexander said, confused. "You were the one who told us we still had things to accomplish."

"Not anymore." Aunt Saffronia shook her head.

"Yup. Our week passes are up." Wil hesitated, looking back at where Edgar waved to them. "Though maybe we could come again?"

"Oh, no," Aunt Saffronia said as they buckled up. "You have too much else to do." But then she surprised them by pointing to a tote bag on the back seat. It was filled with snacks. All the things they loved. She had not only remembered they needed to eat, but remembered what they liked to eat. She offered a small smile before putting her hands on the steering wheel as the engine rumbled to life.

"What else do we have to do?" Theo asked, digging through the snacks even though she was quite full from the churros.

"Listen to them, the children of the night. What music they make . . . ," Aunt Saffronia said, the car drifting into the road.

"We're doing music classes?" Alexander asked.

"Oh, no. You're going to the Sanguine Spa."

"What's that?" Theo asked.

Wil didn't look up from her phone. "A family vacation lodge. In the Little Transylvanian Mountains. It has a five-star rating on . . . Gulp. Gulp again," she muttered.

Aunt Saffronia laughed softly to herself as they drove. "There is a reason why all things are as they are."

Alexander and Theo looked out the window as the trees streaked by impossibly fast. No word from their parents on when they'd return, and now they had another activity to fill up their summer. It couldn't be weirder than Fathoms of Fun had been, and a spa sounded peaceful, at least. Maybe they could rest a little.

Unfortunately for them, the spa wasn't interested in peace, or rest, but perhaps resting in peace was on the agenda. . . .

ACKNOWLEDGMENTS

First and foremost, thanks to the person who wrote the headline that I misread as being about a gothic waterpark. You didn't actually say that, but I couldn't get the idea of a gothic waterpark out of my head. And *now* look what you've done. A whole family's summer, ruined! I hope you're happy with yourself.

Second and secondmost, thanks to the other authors whose words of encouragement and guidance gave me the boost of confidence I needed to throw myself down this metaphorical waterslide of a series: Amie Kaufman, Lindsay Eagar, C. Alexander London, Stephanie Perkins, and Natalie Whipple. You can all borrow my sunscreen any time. Even if you don't ask for it, or want it. I'll keep reminding you. Put on another layer of sunscreen, dear ones.

Third and thirdmost (though the very concept of "most" means there cannot be levels, right? So all these -mosts are the same -most thanks amount), thanks to my agent, Michelle Wolfson, who lets me be just as weird as I want. Thanks to my editor, Wendy Loggia, who helps me figure out the best possible ways to write that weirdness. Thanks to the entire team at Delacorte Press, especially Ali Romig, Hannah Hill, and Lydia Gregovic, as well as stalwart copy editors Colleen Fellingham, Jackie Hornberger, and Alison Kolani, indomitable publicist Kristopher Kam, spookily talented cover designer Carol Ly, and absurdly delightful cover artist Hannah Peck. Really, everyone at Random House Children's Books deserves pie. But not with raisins or meat, because I'm not a monster.

Fifth and fifthmost, I have so many nieces, nephews, and niblings that I can't keep track of how many there are. The other day I looked between the couch cushions for the remote and found another nibling, just waiting for me to give them candy and let them stay up past bedtime. So thanks to all of you for providing me with a very large, legally obligated readership, but especially to Audrey for her early, wide-eyed enthusiasm for the series idea, and to Boston, for helping me name Rodrigo.

Fourth and fourthmost (I went out of order just to tease my poor copy editors, it wasn't even an error, ha ha!), thank you to my own parents for giving us so many memorable summer adventures filled with the joy of freedom tempered only by the sting of an ever-present sunburn reminding us of our own mortality. Childhood is fleeting, memories fade, but Bob Marley on Lake Powell is forever.

Sixth and sixthmost, thank you to my husband and children, who are probably wondering why they're in sixth place, in which case I will ask them to kindly refer to the aside where I very clearly state that all -most is, by very definition, the most, and no -most is more -most than any other -most. But I definitely do love you four the most-est, and I'm very glad to solve mysteries at your sides. Even if most of the mysteries are me shouting "WHO LEFT THEIR CEREAL BOWL ON THE COUNTER RIGHT ABOVE THE DISHWASHER INSTEAD OF JUST PUTTING IT IN THE DISHWASHER." And then the twist is: it was a *ghost*.

Or me. Probably me.

Seventh and seventhmost, thank you to the lifeguards at Magic Waters circa the mid-1990s for being so cute. To the Seven Peaks Waterpark, your lifeguards were not as memorable, but your wave pool still gives me nightmares, which come in very handy as a writer.

And finally, finalmost, to my readers: may your cookies never have raisins, and may all your vacations include churros.

ABOUT THE AUTHOR

Kiersten White has never been a lifeguard, camp counselor, or churro stand operator and in fact has never once experienced summer or summer vacation or solved any mysteries during the aforementioned season. Anyone saying otherwise is lying, and you should absolutely not listen to them, even if they offer you a churro. *Especially* if they offer you a churro.

In addition to never being a lifeguard, camp counselor, or churro stand operator, Kiersten is the *New York Times* bestselling author of more than twenty books, including *Beanstalker and Other Hilarious Scarytales*. She lives with her family near the beach and keeps all her secrets safely buried in her backyard, where they are guarded by a ferocious tortoise named Kimberly.

Visit her at kierstenwhite.com, or look for clues about what awaits the Sinister-Winterbottoms in their next adventures at sinistersummer.com.

JOIN THE SINISTER-WINTERBOTTOMS
ON THEIR NEXT ADVENTURE IN

SINISTER SUMMER

VAMPIRIC VACATION!

Vampiric Vacation excerpt text copyright © 2022 by Kiersten Brazier. Cover art copyright © 2022 by Hannah Peck. Published by Delacorte Press, an imprint of Random House Children's Books, a division of Penguin Random House LLC, New York.

CHAPTER ONE

The day was decidedly sinister.

But not in a charming Sinister-Winterbottom way. If it was a Sinister-Winterbottom way, it might be a day that puttered around the yard building battle robots with built-in cookie ovens, like Mr. Sinister-Winterbottom.

Or it might be a day that painted wild murals of storm-tossed seas populated with tentacled friends while its cookies baked in the battle-robot oven, like Ms. Sinister-Winterbottom.

Or it might be a day with its nose against a phone screen while a frown creased its impressively expressive black eyebrows, like Wilhelmina Sinister-Winterbottom.

Or it might be a day that ran at full speed, the wind whipping its hair, grass lashing its bare shins, screaming joy and delight and something close to anger, like Theodora Sinister-Winterbottom.

Or it might be a day that gazed pensively out the car window at the blurring landscape, wondering what it was heading toward and what might possibly go wrong there because it couldn't imagine that everything would just be fun and pleasant and *nothing* would go wrong, like Alexander Sinister-Winterbottom.

Well . . . on second thought, this day *was* rather like Alexander Sinister-Winterbottom.

Heavy clouds pressed down on the atmosphere, looming closer than clouds ought to loom, as though they were worried about the day, too, and couldn't keep it to themselves. They scooted closer and closer to the earth, peering down at the massive aqua car drifting at alarming speed down a lonely road.

"Pretty dark for noon," Alexander said, unable to swallow the tight lump of worry stuck in his throat. He loved storms—from his own house, curled up on the window seat, with a mug of hot cocoa and a good book, and his mother humming somewhere deep under the house while his father scrambled to get all the battle robots into the garage. But he didn't have his window seat, or hot cocoa, or a good book, or his parents. And he still didn't know why he and his siblings had been banished to spend the summer with their mysterious aunt Saffronia.

Theo repeatedly bonked her head against the cold glass of the car window, like the world's worst drum. She hated long car rides. She couldn't read without getting sick, so she usually listened to an audiobook, but there was no stereo, just a weird old radio you had to adjust by twisting knobs. Aunt Saffronia seemed happy to keep the knobs between stations. The maddening white noise of static filled the car. Every once in a while, Theo could *swear* she heard voices whispering in the static, just barely too quiet to understand.

Which made her mad, because there was already so much she didn't understand right now. Why had their parents woken them in the middle of the night and dumped them on Aunt Saffronia a week ago? Why hadn't their parents at least called since then? Why did she feel both angry and sad at the same time, when she didn't want to feel either, and why did these big feelings make her buzz like she was filled with a hive of angry bees?

Holding her head against the window made her skull vibrate and her teeth chatter. It was as close as she could get to moving while stuck in a car, so she pressed her forehead harder against the glass. This drive seemed like it had lasted forever.

Had they even gone back to Aunt Saffronia's house after leaving Fathoms of Fun Waterpark? Theo glanced at Alexander. He wasn't in his swimsuit, and they were both totally dry. They must have gone back to their aunt's house, showered, and changed. But . . . Theo couldn't remember doing any of that. They had been in the car at Fathoms of Fun, and now they were in the car going somewhere else, and her brain couldn't connect the dots about what had happened between.

"Weird," she muttered, bonking her head once more against the window.

Alexander didn't need to know what Theo thought was weird. Everything was weird, and he didn't like it, and his stomach hurt with all the not-liking he was doing regarding all the weird they were experiencing.

In the passenger seat, Wil, age sixteen and therefore four years older than twins Alexander and Theo, and therefore permanently claiming shotgun in the unfair way older siblings always do—as though a few extra years on earth put them first in line for everything, forever—paused her frantic typing on her phone when a message popped up.

"Edgar," she said, a dreamy smile breaking the intensely focused expression on her face.

"Edgar?" Alexander and Theo said at the same time, perking up. Edgar was a lifeguard at the water park they had just left after a week of fun.

Well . . . after two days of fun. Before the two days of fun were several days of wily Widows, menacing mustaches, terrifying tunnels, and lingering in libraries. Most of their time at Fathoms of Fun had been rather stressful and occasionally scary, thanks to an evil fraternal twin and her henchman. But it ended on a rush of reuniting the real Widows and restoring the park to its Gothic glory. And since it all ended happily, the three Sinister-Winterbottoms only felt happy when they thought of it.

Of course, Wil felt a *little* more than happy when Edgar texted her.

And who could say what Aunt Saffronia felt? Her face was still oddly indistinct, as though seen through several panes of thick glass. Her gaze never seemed to focus on what was around her. Except for right now, as she turned and stared at the antique brass stopwatch Theo still wore around her neck.

"Umm," Alexander said.

"Aunt Saffronia?" Theo added.

"You should be watching the road!" Wil said, which was sharp criticism coming from a girl who never looked up from her phone.

"I should?" Aunt Saffronia tilted her head, her long black hair moving in slow motion, as though she were trapped underwater.

Theo had a strange moment of wondering if Aunt Saffronia really did need to watch the road, though. The car was still going perfectly straight, as though it was steering itself. But that was impossible. A car so old that it didn't even have a good stereo certainly couldn't have a self-driving option . . . could it?

"Please keep your eyes on the road!" Alexander squeaked, a hundred different ways the car could crash all crashing through his head.

Aunt Saffronia laughed, a sound like wind chimes. Not tinkling, bright metal wind chimes, but old chimes, made of wood, so they just sort of brushed and clacked against each other. "Silly boy," she said. "If my eyes were on the road, that would really scare you. I'll keep them in my head." Then she paused, turning ever so slowly to look straight out the windshield. "Unless children like that sort of thing?"

Alexander and Theo exchanged a baffled look. Though they were twins, they were hardly mirror images. Theo had brown hair, cut short so she wouldn't have to worry about brushing it. It was pushed back from her forehead by a headband that made it stick up wildly, rather hedgehoglike in appearance.

Alexander's hair was also cut very short, but not so short that he didn't have to comb it. He still combed it, very carefully, every morning, and often several times during the day. Like Theo, he had brown eyes, and freckles across his nose. Unlike Theo's, his knees were not covered in bruises and scars, and also unlike Theo, he had managed to spend an entire week at a water park and not get sunburned at all. His white skin was still very white.

Theo, meanwhile, scratched her shoulders, where a sunburn nagged at her.

Wil was also not sunburned, her brown skin perfectly protected since she spent most of the time at the water park doing the same thing she did with most of her time everywhere else: gazing at Rodrigo, her beloved phone.

Though, increasingly, it looked like what Rodrigo's small screen showed her didn't make her happy. Already the smile at a text from Edgar was gone, replaced with a frustrated frown as she idly tugged on one of her many long braids. If their father were here, he would gently remind Wil not to pull her hair.

But their father wasn't here, so Wil's hair had no one to look out for it.

"Where are we going?" Theo asked. "And when will we get there? And when are our parents coming to get us?"

"And aren't we going to stop at the house to pick up our things? Or is this just a day trip? Or are we going to meet our parents?" Alexander couldn't help but sound hopeful at that last question.

Unfortunately, Aunt Saffronia was very good at only hearing the questions she wanted to hear. "We aren't finished yet."

"With the drive? Or the vacation?" Alexander asked, desperate for some sort of clarity. All he remembered about being dropped off with Aunt Saffronia was that it had been in the middle of the night. His mom was trying hard to sound cheery, but her eyes were worried, and his father had been hastily packing several of his most impressive robots. They had also, for some reason, lit a lot of candles in a circle. And that was it.

Since then, the only contact they'd had with their parents was a letter left in Alexander's luggage. His mom had a way of packing that was like magic—every time Alexander opened the suitcase, he found exactly what he needed, whether it was an extra pair of board shorts, or his softest sleep shirt, or extra floss, because cavities never take a summer vacation. So when Alexander had found the letter from his mom, he'd thought it was what he needed: Answers. Explanations. A scavenger hunt that would end with his being reunited with his parents.

Instead, he had found a letter telling him to be cautious, Theo to be brave, and Wil to use her phone. All it had said about Aunt Saffronia was that they should listen to her, except when they shouldn't. And something about gathering tools. Which seemed weird, since they weren't at home with their dad, who was forever losing his robot-building materials.

Alexander sighed, feeling squeezed by impending stormy doom. Aunt Saffronia wasn't going to tell him anything. She was just like most adults, barreling through the world, never explaining the baffling things going on around them.

Theo didn't give up on answers so easily. Maybe if she broke the sentences down, one question at a time, it would help Aunt Saffronia. Sometimes if a teacher gave Theo too many instructions at once, she couldn't figure out which task to do first, so she ended up doing none of them and instead building an elaborate tower out of pencils, glue sticks, and erasers. Her mom was really good at helping Theo organize her brain, which only had one speed: *fast*.

But she would slow it down to try to get answers from Aunt Saffronia.

"Where are we?" Theo asked.

"In the car." Aunt Saffronia sighed worriedly. "They told me you children were bright, that you could do this, but sometimes I wonder. It's a lot to ask of any child, much less one who can't understand when she's inside a car."

Theo resisted the urge to tug on her own hair. "Where are we going?"

"Nowhere," Aunt Saffronia said. "We're already here." The car stopped abruptly. It had been moving so fast that the landscape was a blur, and now it was stopped, and none of the three children could remember the jolt, or even the gradual slowing. But that was quickly forgotten by the alarm they felt at what they were reading. Usually reading was a pleasant task for Alexander and Theo, but it didn't feel pleasant as they looked at the sign in front of them:

WELCOME TO THE LITTLE TRANSYLVANIAN MOUNTAINS
WE ARE DYING TO MEET YOU